FIVE GRAVES WEST

Dave Drury was a man with a past he believed long forgotten. But then an old enemy thought he would cash in on this knowledge. What he had forgotten, though, was that Drury made his own rules and those who crossed the line could expect sudden death. And anyone who thought Drury would be at a disadvantage in the murderous Altar Desert overlooked the fact that Dave was the only white man alive who had crossed it. Soon there would be deadly violence . . .

Books by Tyler Hatch
in the Linford Western Library:

A LAND TO DIE FOR
BUCKSKIN GIRL
DEATHWATCH TRAIL
LONG SHOT
VIGILANTE MARSHAL

TYLER HATCH

FIVE GRAVES
WEST

Complete and Unabridged

LINFORD
Leicester

First published in Great Britain in 2001 by
Robert Hale Limited
London

First Linford Edition
published 2003
by arrangement with
Robert Hale Limited
London

The moral right of the author has been asserted

British Library CIP Data

Hatch, Tyler
    Five graves west.—Large print ed.—
Linford western library
1. Western stories
2. Large type books
I. Title
823.9'14 [F]

ISBN 0–7089–9974–3

Published by
F. A. Thorpe (Publishing)
Anstey, Leicestershire

Set by Words & Graphics Ltd.
Anstey, Leicestershire
Printed and bound in Great Britain by
T. J. International Ltd., Padstow, Cornwall

This book is printed on acid-free paper

1

Dead Men

The train came down through the high pass into lashing rain and the danger of a wash-out on the line.

The man peering through the window of the rear door of the last car rubbed away some of the condensation so that he could see more clearly. It was no good: he would have to step out onto the platform so that he could look along the train and see what was waiting below.

It was cold and windy and he cursed, squinted into a gust of rain, lifting a gnarled hand to shade his eyes. There was the high trestle bridge below and about half a mile ahead. He could see the blur of whitewater beneath, surging around the heavy wooden supports. It seemed higher than usual which meant the rivers were up and that could indicate that the flat country beyond the bridge was already under water.

The man swore and ducked back into the warmth of the car. A second man lounging in a doorway beyond, turned incuriously to look over the shoulder.

'Rainin' outside is it, Cole?'

'Very funny. Looks like there could be floods.'

The second man straightened. 'Damn! How's that affect us?'

The drenched man wiped off his six-gun with his kerchief and shrugged. 'Don't — if we move fast.'

'Fast wasn't planned for!'

'So change the plan to fit the conditions. Ready?'

'Aw hell, wait-up! I dunno about this, Cole!'

Cole sighed. 'Well, you've had plenty time to think about it. You dunno now, you're never gonna know.' The six-gun rammed against the startled man's midriff and Cole dropped hammer.

The shot was muffled, though by no means silenced, and the guard was blown back into the lantern-lit car beyond, doubled over, his mouth sagging and already dribbling blood as he straightened convulsively and then collapsed in the narrow aisle between the seats.

There were half a dozen men seated in the car. They all turned sharply at the gun shot — in time to see the two men in the rear seats shot in the back of the head by the man called Cole.

'*Madre de Dios*!' exclaimed the slim Mexican in the general's uniform, leaping to his feet and crossing himself, his dark skin turning sallow as he stared wide-eyed at the man called Cole.

The American spread his arms, shaking his head.

'She won't help you none, Carlos, old man . . . Sorry about that but . . . ' Cole smiled crookedly, gunwhipped a small, big-bellied Mexican on his left as the man half rose out of his seat, clawing at the pistol in his waistband.

The Mexican sprawled in the aisle and Cole kicked him in the head for

3

good measure as he stepped over him. The tall Mexican named Carlos stared, slack-mouthed.

'But — you are supposed to *guard* me!'

Cole shrugged, smiling crookedly. 'They offered more *dinero*, Carlos. Sorry, *amigo*, but you know how it is.' He turned his gaze to the *Americano* moving behind Carlos now, gun in hand. He nodded and Carlos started to turn in alarm, but the gun barrel caught him across the side of the head and he grunted as he fell to his knees, dazed. The American hit him again and Cole turned to the last remaining Mexican who had been seated beside Carlos.

'Tell your boss he can't have Carlos yet awhile, Juan — Montegas needs to — talk to him first.'

The Mexican was slim and quite young and he lifted dark, glittering eyes from the sprawled form at his feet.

'You will die for this!' he hissed.

'Man's gotta die sometime for some reason — but I'll die rich.'

4

'But you *will* die!'

Cole's sneer faded and his grey eyes grew ugly as he looked at the young Mexican. 'You know — we don't really need you to give anyone any kind of a message, Juan. They'll soon figure out what's happened to Carlos, who has him. Which means we got no use for you now.'

Cole's six-gun roared and Juan was blown backwards so that his body hung over the edge of a seat, twitching. The man kneeling beside Carlos, finishing tying his hands behind his back, frowned up at Cole.

'More dead bodies than we figured on.'

'Bigger share for us.' Cole reloaded swiftly. 'C'mon, Con, sling Carlos over your shoulder and get ready to jump. We'll be across the bridge in a couple of minutes.'

'I sure as hell hope the others are waitin'!' Con said, grunting a little as he settled the unconscious Carlos across his broad shoulders.

'Well, if they ain't we've got a long walk ahead of us.'

Con, on his way down the aisle, stopped dead, staring. 'You're kiddin'!'

Cole stared at him levelly, eyebrows arched and just as Con started to cuss, smiled abruptly and opened the door out onto the rain-lashed platform.

' 'Course I'm kidding! They ain't there we might as well put a bullet in Carlos's head — then another, in our own . . . Ain't no way we can walk away from this one, Con. It either works or we're dead — '

'Thanks a lot! That cheers me up no end!'

Cole chuckled. 'Figured it might. OK, here we go and relax. There're the boys waiting with the hosses in the trees across the bridge . . . Told you we'd all die rich!'

★　★　★

The card game was going on in a smoke-heavy corner of the saloon when

Cole Fisher came in from the heat and glaring sunlight. His horse was standing at the hitch rail, head drooping, powdered with alkali as was its rider, weary and no doubt thirsty and hungry.

Just like Cole Fisher. But he aimed to tend to his own needs first: the damn horse could wait. It had thrown him twice out in the desert, run off when he tried to mount it this morning, so it could blame well wait and nobody better say anything about it.

He was a solid man, Cole Fisher, big through chest and shoulders, almost neckless, his large, round head seeming to balance there of its own accord. He thumbed back his hat and a trickle of alkali hazed the air about his face. He coughed irritably as he lifted the hat, ran his fingers through his shock of wheat-coloured hair and threw the hat on the bar. He tossed a silver dollar onto the dusty crown as a barkeep sauntered across and said,

'Let me know when that runs out.'

'Two shots'll do it,' the 'keep told

him and he didn't flinch from the murderous look Fisher threw his way. His face was lined and battered and scarred. It was a face that had had just about everything happen to it over the years and the owner no longer cared.

'Expensive damn rotgut!' Fisher snapped, turning a few heads of other drinkers.

But not the card players: they were all concentrating on their hands, busy with the process of raising bets, a couple of men tossing in their cards.

'There's another saloon right down the street,' the barkeep said and began to turn away.

Fisher grabbed his arm, felt the iron sinews and eased his grip a mite. He forced a grin. 'I'm too thirsty to go hunt up another saloon. Gimme a shot. And if you got some steak and potatoes . . . ?'

'We got 'em. Cost you another silver dollar.'

Fisher swore and dug out another coin. As the barman poured his shot and moved away, a voice was raised at the card table.

'Hey!' The word dropped into the saloon's murmur like a gunshot, stilling all conversation and laughter, bringing every head there around towards the poker game. A thin man, who looked like he had a pigeon chest underneath the grimy, frayed shirt-front showing under his shiny-cloth coat, crashed his chair over as he stood up, one hand pointing a bony finger at one of the players. 'You slipped that last card from the bottom of the deck!'

The silence was heavy, pulsing. No one moved, no one spoke. Eyes swivelled to the accused player.

He looked like a cowhand, maybe a hardrock rancher in for a few drinks and a little relaxation. His clothes were average, patched on the shirt pocket, stained dark with sweat and still having a maguey thorn caught on one shoulder. His trousers were mostly hidden by the leather chaps he wore and the six-gun holstered on his right thigh seemed to be there because it was a handy tool, rather than a weapon to settle trouble. His face was squarish, the cheekbones prominent, the left one twisted a little with a writhe of scar tissue. The nose was largish, battered slightly to starboard and the mouth was hard to see beneath the brown frontier moustache.

But the eyes were clear, blue-green, steady on the face of the man who was pointing at him.

Funny, thought Fisher, none of the other card players had moved since the tinhorn had made the accusation. It told Fisher something about the man with the blue-green eyes.

He was either totally innocent of cheating and the others knew it — or he was well able to take care of any tinhorn loco enough to fling such a charge in his face.

'Sit down, Luke,' the man said, thumbing back his hat so that his rugged face was fully revealed in the dusty sunlight coming through the narrow window. 'We all know you're losing and haven't enough to cover your bets, but this is no way out of it . . .'

'You're a goddamn liar, Drury!' the tinhorn shouted and if that silence in the saloon could have gotten any deeper than it already was, well, it would've plunged clean through the floor.

For a moment there the silence actually *hurt*.

Then Drury stood, lazily, no belligerence in his movements or on his face.

'Luke, you run off at the mouth too much. You been caught out this time, but you've picked the wrong man for your cover-up. Now, take your hand away from the edge of your coat and sit down and we'll talk it over. It's too damn hot to get into any kind of a wrangle.'

'Too damn hot? Or you're too damn yellow!'

Well, that was it: a man can take just so much and he draws his own lines. Someone eventually steps over them and if he's his own man, he just has to do something about it.

'Damn you, Luke, I was just enjoying this game, too!'

Luke had already started his draw, his left hand whipping open his coat, right streaking to the holstered pistol under his left arm.

Drury made his move — and it surprised the hell out of Cole Fisher who was watching closely from where he stood at the bar.

Drury's six-gun was holstered on his right thigh, butt to the back, in the normal way most men carried their Colts. But . . . *the man's right hand streaked across his body to his left hip, at waist level, hand snatching for a gun anchored for a cross-draw . . . But there was no gun there!*

By then, the tinhorn had his gun free and the hammer was coming back. Drury realized he had made the wrong move, grabbed the edge of the table and men dived for the floor. Money and cards scattered as he heaved the scarred pine into Luke.

The tinhorn staggered, spinning away, then twisted back with a swift, almost snakelike movement, his gun coming up and blasting. He got off two shots — one banging into the wall beside the window, the second chewing splinters out of the ceiling as he fired while he was falling backwards.

Drury was crouched with his smoking Colt in his right hand and Fisher whistled softly through his teeth. *Goddamnit! He'd been actually watching Drury and damned if he'd seen the man's draw after he heaved the table into Luke . . . His draw must have been like a lightning bolt striking!*

Luke was down and writhing and kicking, his gun skidding along the sawdusted floorboards. Someone stood on it so he couldn't lift it again, but Luke was no longer interested in the gun. All he wanted to do was get to a sawbones . . .

'Damn you, Luke!' snapped Drury, gun back in holster now.

Then the batwings slapped open and

the law arrived, hatless, clutching a six-gun, looking around wildly. He stopped dead when he saw Luke on the floor — and Drury standing over him, right hand resting on the butt of his holstered gun.

'Judas priest!' breathed the sheriff, a middle-aged man, a little out of shape judging by the way he was breathing. 'You din' do it, did you, Dave?'

Drury spread his hands helplessly.

'Luke was losing and figured the best way out was to accuse someone of cheating.'

The sheriff nodded gently. 'And the fool picked you! You should've killed him and done everyone a favour.'

Fisher was curious: it looked like this Drury was quite well respected around here. It was obvious the sheriff didn't doubt his story, waved aside the other card players who backed up Drury's version.

Cole Fisher turned as the barkeep brought his plate of steak and potatoes and slapped it on the bar. As the man started away, Fisher said,

'This Drury's mighty fast on the draw.'

'Seems so.'

Cole Fisher frowned. 'Sounds like you never seen him do it before.'

'That's right, friend . . . Dave Drury ain't never been in trouble in the five, six years he's been here. Oh, he might've had a brawl or two when he was cuttin' loose, but that's normal. Far as I know that's the first time that gun of his has cleared leather in all that time.'

'Well, I'll be damned! Say, you notice how he sort of made as if to draw his gun from his other hip . . . ? Before he kicked that table into the tinhorn, I mean . . .'

The barkeep's scared eyes bored into Fisher. 'No. I never noticed nothin' like that — An' if I did, I'd keep it to myself. Dave Drury's business is his own.'

Fisher didn't push it, but after eating and buying a couple of drinks — by that time, Luke had been taken out by the sheriff to a sawbones — Cole Fisher had a better picture of this man Drury.

In fact, he studied the man long and covertly, boring his gaze into that rugged face, looking away quickly when Drury sensed his interest and glanced up from a new game of cards . . .

Fisher left the saloon abruptly, his mind made up. He went to the town's other saloons and into the general store and the livery. In each case he managed to bring Dave Drury into the conversation and he learned a good deal more about the man.

Happy with his efforts, Fisher found his way to the telegraph office half-way along Main.

He wrote out his message on the usual yellow form. Addressed to *J. Santiago, Cimarron Valley, New Mexico*.

The message was brief:

FOUND HIM. READY WHEN YOU ARE. COLE.

2

A Man Called Kincaid

Woody Maguire pushed his hat back from his forehead, tore off his neckerchief and wiped away the sweat. All without taking his eyes off Dave Drury who was lounging against an upright at the top of the short flight of steps leading to the house porch, rolling a cigarette.

'So Luke finally got to you?'

Drury licked the paper, twirled it into a cylinder and placed it between his lips before answering.

'Full of rotgut and on a losing streak. I heard he got kicked out of his room, too. He was ripe to push things to the limit.'

'Should've killed him. The man's a fool. What's happenin' about him now?'

Drury shrugged as he lit the cigarette, shook out the vesta and flicked it over the rail into the ranch yard.

'Sheriff's putting him on a train out of town when he recovers.'

Maguire, a man in his forties, nodded, mopped his face once more and adjusted his hat. 'County'll be a better place for it — Pity you had to drag iron on him, though.'

Drury blew smoke and lifted his gaze to Maguire's tanned, weathered face. 'You dunno all of it yet. It's been so long since I had to go for a six-gun I forgot where I was wearing it.'

Maguire straightened, frowning, trying to figure out what Drury was saying. 'You mean you . . . ?'

Drury nodded. 'Yeah. Started a cross-draw . . . Luke damn near nailed me.'

Maguire pursed his lips in a silent whistle. 'Think anyone noticed?'

'Well, plenty in the bar *saw* it, but what they made of it I wouldn't know.'

'Ah, they won't connect it with anything. Like you said, it's been a long time since you had to slap leather in a hurry. Never before in this town . . . Anyone say anythin'?'

Dave Drury shook his head. 'It was a fool thing to do, though.'

'Split-second move. Instinctive. You spent a lot of years packin' iron on that left hip, butt to the fore . . . '

Drury straightened and adjusted his work-stained hat. 'Ah, well, to hell with it. We better start rounding up those mavericks in Papago Canyon, get a brand on 'em.'

'Got Mel and Grady started on a holdin' corral. I'll have Cooky make us up some grubsacks and we can leave this afternoon. Suit you?'

'I guess.'

Drury went into the house and Woody Maguire frowned after him. He knew the signs, the way his partner and boss was moving with that slow, slouching gait that most folk thought was part of his easy-going nature.

But Maguire knew better: it told him Drury had things on his mind. And he'd bet it was something else besides how many mavericks they were going to pop out of the brush of Papago Canyon.

That move for a cross-draw could spoil everything if anyone thought hard about it and did a little wondering.

There was no use anybody kidding themselves about it, either. Trouble could well be a-brewing for Dave Drury.

★ ★ ★

'It was that hand driving across his belly for a gun-butt that wasn't there that made me look twice.'

Cole Fisher was speaking animatedly as he strode away from the Tucson railroad siding beside the tall, swarthy man in the split-tail coat and new-looking hat. Jason Santiago was smoking a cheroot and he squinted his dark brown eyes against the smoke as he turned his head to look down at Cole Fisher. Santiago was tall, looked slim but was taut-muscled and fit. He was about forty, in his prime, strode along with easy, distance-eating strides, Fisher alongside him, followed by two more gun-hung men and a Mexican pushing a handcart loaded with luggage.

'Plenty men used to a cross-draw could make that mistake,' Santiago said, his slight accent giving his speech a pleasant sound. He drew on his cheroot. 'You brought me down here, Cole. It damn well better not be for nothing.'

Cole Fisher shrugged; plenty of men would shake in their boots if Jason Santiago spoke to them like that, but not Fisher. He was afraid of no man.

'I took a damn good look at him, Jace, and you take away that moustache he's sporting, and you drop five years off . . . makes him about the right age and the time's right for when he first showed-up here. Had money to buy himself a ranch west of here. Not doing so well, but he gets along pretty good with folk here-abouts. They say he's responsible for stopping the Indian raids on this here town.'

Santiago frowned, slowed his pace. 'How did he do that?'

'Word is he showed up with an old Apache tagging along and seems the Injun was some old-time chief and still carried a lot of weight with the local tribes. Drury and him powwowed with the Injuns and somehow set things to rights. He won himself a lot of friends.'

Jason Santiago stopped, dropped his cheroot and ground the smouldering butt into the ground, swinging his head towards Fisher.

'He sounds — interesting, this Drury. I wonder what his price is . . . ?'

Fisher's look was sharp, but as he was about to speak, Santiago started forward again and Cole began walking.

Let the man find out for himself whether Drury was the kind of man who could be bought.

* * *

The four riders were mighty weary when they drove the mavericks in from

Papago Canyon.

They were powdered with dust, beard-shagged, aching from long days in the saddle.

'Visitors,' called Maguire hoarsely, pointing to the strange horses in the smaller of the two corrals in the yard.

'An' makin' 'emselves to home, looks like,' growled Mel Roberts, a broken-nosed cowpoke who was more at home in a saddle than any bed he'd ever seen.

'Someone on the porch, Dave,' allowed lanky Grady Timms, pointing. 'One looks like a Mex!'

Drury said nothing, hawked up some dust out of his throat, spat, glanced at Maguire and the two of them rode on ahead, cutting across the home pasture towards the distant shingle-roofed house they all called home in this part of Arizona. Mel and Grady Timms continued to haze the bunch of mavericks towards the holding corrals.

There were four men on the porch when Drury and Maguire rode into the yard and dismounted swiftly. One was a

Mexican, or part-Mex, anyway, tall, too, six-four or -five. There was a beefy man with yellow hair and a ball-like head beside him and Maguire, hitching at his gunbelt, happened to catch the expression which flickered across Drury's face when he saw the big man.

It was wary, with just a touch of alarm. But the man covered so fast that Maguire wasn't sure. The other two men looked tough, hard *hombres* that you could find along the border and buy for a few bucks.

Altogether, a group to be leery of, leastways, until you found out what they wanted.

It was the Mexican who spoke, stepping out of the shade into the burning sunlight, hatless, jet-black hair carefully in place and glistening. His teeth were very white as he smiled.

'Mr Dave Drury?' There was very little accent.

The rancher nodded, wondering why the Mexican directed the question at him — as if he already had a description but just wanted to make sure.

'I hope you don't mind us making ourselves at home, Mr Drury, but we arrived last night and there was no one here to ask permission to stay. Your cook wouldn't commit himself but we figured to wait a day or so, hoping you'd turn up.'

'You could've camped in the barn,' Drury said quietly and Jason Santiago's smile widened.

'I'm a man who likes his comfort, Mr Drury — and, of course, I am prepared to pay for it.'

Drury recognized it as a ploy to test his mercenary attitudes and he shrugged. 'There'll be no charge — unless something's got broken.'

Santiago shook his head quickly.

'We will pay for the food we've eaten, of course. Your cook prepared us a reasonable meal.'

'Forget about the money. What d'you want?'

Santiago arched his thin but very

dark eyebrows. 'A man who gets straight to the point, I see.'

Drury said nothing and Santiago introduced himself, then the yellow-haired man as Cole Fisher, the hard-eyed *hombre* with the flat, Indian-like face as Con Conrads, and the fourth man, of medium height but thick about the middle and with a receding jaw, simply as 'Quick'. Santiago laughed at the puzzled expression on Drury's face.

'Not 'quick' because of his intellect, but because of certain other talents, you understand.'

'I understand,' allowed Drury coolly and introduced Maguire as his fore-man.

'Foreman?' echoed Cole Fisher. 'On a place this size? You got big notions, Kincaid.'

The air itself seemed to go very still at the sound of the name. Woody Maguire snapped his head towards Drury while Drury himself stiffened, but kept his face carefully blank. His blue-green eyes drilled into Fisher's grey ones.

'Must have dust clogging your ears, friend. Name's Drury, Dave Drury.'

Fisher smiled, tugged at one thickened earlobe.

'Yeah, so they tell me in town. But I seen you down that tinhorn a few nights back and you kind of reminded me of a feller I used to know up on the Yellowstone. Name of Kincaid — Brock Kincaid. He was a lieutenant in the cavalry. I was scouting for the army at the time.'

Drury said nothing and Cole frowned, glancing at Santiago, not sure how to continue. The tall man worked up a smile. But it was a little tight at the edges.

'It would seem to be a case of mistaken identity, Cole.'

Fisher looked at Drury.

'Nah. I never forget a face. This Kincaid never wore a moustache when I knew him but he sure looks like you — even to that little twisted scar on your left cheekbone. Sioux arrow, weren't it?'

Still Drury said nothing and Fisher sighed.

'Yeah, it was a Sioux arrow, battle of Black Bear Creek. Ricocheted from a rock, passed clear through the neck of a trooper and hit you a glancing blow. Lucky it didn't take your eye out.'

Another awkward silence.

'This Kincaid sounds lucky,' allowed Santiago. 'How is your luck running these days, Mr er — Drury?'

Dave Drury waved a hand around the parched looking dusty yard and the brown pastures beyond.

'See for yourself. A long, dry season and no sign of rain yet. To be a success, a rancher needs better luck than that, Mr Santiago.'

'Mmmmm . . . perhaps I can help you out of your difficulties. Would two thousand dollars be useful?'

Maguire whistled softly, snapping his gaze towards Drury.

'Lot of money, Dave.'

'Too much for it to be for anything honest,' opined Drury and Santiago lost his smile.

'You are a cynic, Mr Drury. Let us dispense with all this sniping and insinuations. Let us put our cards face up on the table. I believe you like card games?'

'Only honest ones.'

Santiago's eyes narrowed.

'That word again. Well, Cole will tell you a story first, not a long one, I promise. In fact, you may already know it, but allow him to finish anyway, please.'

Drury and Maguire pushed their way up onto the crowded porch and found a section of rail to sit on. By now, Mel and Grady were driving the mavericks into the large corral, looking towards the house, ready to come at Drury's signal.

'This feller Kincaid,' Cole Fisher began, hooking his thick thumbs through his slanted gun-belt. 'There was some army money missing, details don't matter. Thing is, 'most everyone knew he was innocent, but they framed him to protect the real thief — who just happened to be a colonel's nephew. Kincaid never had a chance. He'd been in charge of payroll escorts, see, had keys to the money-chests. They gave him seven years in Leavenworth Stockade, Kansas.'

Santiago watched Drury's impassive face. The silence grew deeper. There was no reply from Dave Drury and Fisher continued:

'When Kincaid got out, I guess he figured the army owed him something — and I don't blame him. I'd feel the same way. Well, seems the army being the army, sticklers for routine, still shipped their payrolls at the same time by the same route even after seven years. This was up in Wyoming, where Kincaid had been stationed before his court martial. Seems he managed to rob one of them payrolls, and then headed down the old Outlaw Trail clear into Mexico. They say he likely had

30

help, someone to show him the trail, but in any case he made it across the border. At that time, Mexico wanted something from the good ol' US and they cooperated and agreed to hunt for Kincaid, allowed a couple of US army officers and yours truly, me being a top tracker, in to help.'

'Mighty unusual,' allowed Maguire.

'Well, the army wanted Kincaid real bad: he was thumbing his nose at 'em, you see.'

Fisher smiled.

'Anyway, we picked up Kincaid's trail although he'd covered it pretty well and crowded him into the Altar Desert in north-west Mexico, Sonora way. No white man had ever crossed it alive and we knew we had him then. But Kincaid disappeared, so we figured he must've died out there — and the money was gone for ever.'

Fisher shook his head.

'Never did set easy with me. I knew Kincaid was a smart *hombre* and it didn't seem like one of his moves to be so stupid as to let himself get pushed into a killer desert like the Altar . . . '

'Tough man, this Kincaid,' Drury said quietly and Cole Fisher smiled widely. 'By the sounds of things.'

'Mebbe. But I found out later he was travelling with an old Apache he'd picked up along the way. This Apache, called Crooked Tree, had been one of a wild bunch that made raids up into Arizona and then ran back into Sonora and hid out till they felt like making another raid for white man's goods. He spent a lot of time down there, and Kincaid had been stationed along the border at one time. I figure this Apache led Kincaid safely across that Altar Desert and he made his way north into Arizona. You know there ain't much of a population down in the south-west, was even less five, six years ago when Brock Kincaid arrived . . . '

Cole Fisher shouldered off the wall, linked his fingers and cracked his knuckles, at the same time loosening his arms. He gave the rancher a crooked grin.

'Dunno what happened to the Apache but I figured a few things out and I reckon Kincaid calls himself Dave Drury now . . . That pretty close to what happened, Lieutenant . . . ?'

Still Drury didn't speak and Fisher's smile widened.

'One other thing. This Kincaid, used to wearing his pistol army-fashion, I guess, packed his six-gun the same way — without a flap on the holster, of course — after he got out of the stockade. Developed a mighty fast draw and got himself a reputation going down the Outlaw Trail. They say he killed fourteen men making his escape. That right, Lieutenant?'

Drury held the man's mocking gaze for a long minute and then said very quietly,

'Not if you count the Apache — I killed him, too.'

3

Blood Contract

If Drury wasn't the centre of attention before, he sure was now after that statement.

Woody Maguire frowned at him, a trace of uncertainty in his look. Santiago, Fisher and the others watched the rancher closely and Cole Fisher smiled crookedly.

'You turned out to be a real dyed-in-the-wool badman after all, eh, Lieutenant?'

'Blame Leavenworth,' Drury said flatly.

'You admit then that you are Brock Kincaid?' Santiago wanted it all spelled out and laid on the table so there could be no mistake.

'I'm Dave Drury. Brock Kincaid is dead. He died out in that desert. The army thinks he's dead, the Mexicans think he's dead, just about everyone thinks he's dead.'

'But we know different.' Jason Santiago sounded smug, confident.

The rancher gave him a hard look.

'Question is, what're you aiming to do with that knowledge?'

Santiago's teeth flashed whitely.

'Come now, Lieutenant Kincaid! What do you *think* I'm going to do with it?'

'Drury, not Kincaid. Well, I reckon you're gonna blackmail me into something. Or maybe you want a share of the payroll, but I'm here to tell you there ain't much left. Most of it went on the ranch and stocking it up and there's been a few bad seasons . . . '

Santiago shook his head. 'The payroll doesn't interest us, except as something to pin down your true identity.'

'Well, whatever your reason, I can raise a few men in a very short time that could prevent your ever leaving here and making use of that information. As soon as we saw your horses I sent one of my men to a neighbouring spread and he'll be back right soon with a bunch of armed men — something we worked out amongst ourselves living down here in more or less isolation. Indians aren't a worry any longer, but occasionally we have a bunch of hardcases come through who figure because we're out here on our own they can ride roughshod over us.'

Santiago smiled crookedly, glancing at Cole Fisher.

'I think he bluffs, Cole.'

'Damn sure of it. Con was watching from the rise and he seen four men hazing in them mavericks. No one left.'

'Well, stick around and we'll see,' Drury said easily.

Santiago sighed. 'My friend, you begin to weary me. Long before I made the journey to Tucson I took certain precautions. Briefly, Cole's suspicions about your true identity were outlined in a notarized document left with an attorney a long way from Tucson. If he does not receive a telegraph message from us, worded in a specific way within a certain time, the document will be passed along to the army. Now you know, whether they believe it or not, they *will* be bound to investigate. You understand?'

The rancher nodded gently, his blue-green gaze holding to Santiago's, leanly handsome face.

'A professional blackmailer . . . '

The tall Mexican didn't like that but although his face darkened he said nothing.

'All right. No more beating about the bush. Tell me what you want.'

'First, my offer of two thousand dollars is increased to five thousand. The smaller amount was just to see if money could claim your interest.'

'Five thousand would get most men's attention.'

'Of course. You would expect to work hard to earn that amount, wouldn't you?'

'Uh-huh,' Drury said, the sound barely audible. Maguire moved uneasily but the rancher didn't look at him.

Cole Fisher had a smirk on his face as he watched closely. Con Conrads and the man called Quick merely watched alertly, keeping their hands close to gun-butts.

'You will be required to break the law.'

'Already figured that.'

Jason Santiago held up a hand briefly.

'Don't get me wrong, Kincaid — er — Drury. There will be nothing so crude as a robbery involved. But it will be a serious breach of the law.'

'Mexican or American?'

Santiago arched his eyebrows. 'Perhaps I can best answer by saying a little of both. Does that bother you?'

Dave Drury shrugged.

Santiago studied him for a spell, took out a cheroot from a leather case and Fisher struck a vesta and held it for him.

'You have heard of General Carlos Herrera?'

Drury nodded. 'Rebel leader who overthrew Patero's government a couple of years back, made himself unofficial *el Presidente* for a short time. But he was betrayed by one of his *commandantes*, Montegas, and Herrera had to run for the border, supposedly with the help of a US senator, but was kidnapped from his special train . . . That was about three months ago. I'd say he's dead by now — or wishing he was.'

'He is still alive,' Santiago said firmly, his face very serious, mouth tight. 'He is my uncle.'

'What do you expect me to do?'

'To rescue him. The plan at present includes a crossing of the Desert Altar. You've already done it once.'

'I had help that time: the old Apache, Crooked Tree.'

'The one you killed,' said Cole Fisher sardonically. 'Or did you?'

'I did, but it was this way, Cole: a mountain lion jumped him, tore him up real bad, gutted him. Helluva mess. I owed him a lot more than a quick bullet, but all I could do was put him out of his misery.'

Fisher looked disappointed and Drury smiled crookedly. 'And it wasn't four-teen men, Cole. It was three . . . and they were outlaws trying to take the payroll off me.'

'Gospel?'

'Gospel,' the rancher assured him and Fisher swore softly.

'Well, you know, I had trouble believing that even after seven years in the stockade you'd turned out to be such a cold-blooded killer! I've seen you save a half-dozen Injun kids on cavalry raids. Once it was a squaw . . . ' He shook his head slowly. 'So you ain't the murdering son of a bitch folk reckon after all.' He turned to Santiago. 'This might call for a change of plan, Jace.'

'I think not.' Santiago eyed Drury hard. 'He has built a good life for himself here. I don't think he wants it destroyed by his past being revealed.

People will still believe he killed fourteen men just to keep that payroll, no matter what he claims. In any case, he would face the gallows, not just a few more years in Leavenworth.'

Dave Drury took out his tobacco-sack and papers, noting the way Quick and Con straightened and their hands tightened about their gun-butts. They watched closely while he made a cigarette and fumbled a vesta out of a shirt pocket. He blew smoke in their direction, waiting for Santiago to continue.

'I think you are a very tough man, Lieutenant Kincaid — Oh, don't worry, I will refer to you as 'Drury' from now on as you wish but only if you do as *I* wish. Fair enough, eh? What I want you to do is to rescue my uncle and to take him across the Desert Altar to the Gulf of California where a boat will be waiting. For this I will pay you five thousand American dollars in gold.'

Santiago's neat moustache twitched as he smiled and said, quite affably, 'Or you may choose the alternative.'

Later that afternoon, when Maguire and Drury were alone for a time, while Santiago's group still sprawled at their ease on the porch, Woody said, 'You gonna do what he wants?'

'You know what'll happen if I don't.'

'Hell, we can convince folk you never killed no fourteen men! I can swear them outlaws tried to jump you and you downed them in self-defence. Don't go backwards, Dave! You've worked too hard to get where you are now . . . '

'There's something else, Woody. I owe Carlos Herrera.'

'How the hell you know him?' Maguire was genuinely surprised.

'When I was on the dodge, in Durango — he was leader of the rebels then and he hid me out, gave me time to recover from the wounds I got in the shoot-out with those outlaws . . . '

'Well, knowin' how you don't like to be beholden, I guess you'll do your best to bust Herrera out then.'

'Don't see I have much choice.'

'Reckon Santiago'll come up with the five thousand?'

'Now that's something I'm just going to have to wait and find out.'

'That Fisher has anythin' to say about it, it'll be a bullet in the back of the head . . . ' Maguire frowned. 'Why ain't Montegas killed Herrera long before this, anyway?'

'They say he's broke so he's likely hoping for finance from the US, and Washington won't stand for political murder on our doorstep. Besides, if Herrera dies in a political prison, it'll make a martyr out of him and cause even more trouble for Montegas . . . '

'Well, I guess I can see what you mean. But in that case, you might be doin' Montegas a favour in grabbin' Herrera. I mean, that desert's a real killer an' if he dies — '

'Yeah, it occurred to me that we've only got Santiago's word for it that the general's his uncle . . . '

'Which prison they got Herrera in?'

'The big one at Hermosillo in Sonora according to Santiago. Montegas is planning to move him to Caborca on the edge of the desert because the talk is Herrera's old rebel bunch is gathering again and Montegas is afraid they'll try to bust him out. Caborca's built like a fortress. I guess Montegas wants to make sure Herrera stays put.'

Maguire whistled softly. 'Nothin' like a nice easy job. Guess we'll just have to grab him somewhere between Hermosillo and Caborca?'

Drury looked at him sharply. 'You don't have to buy into this, Woody . . . '

'Showed you the way down the Outlaw Trail, din' I? And you gave me a share in this ranch when I was down and out . . . I don't run out on anyone treats me decent like you done, Dave!'

'Woody, I'll be mighty glad to have your help but . . . you gotta savvy we might not get out of this alive.'

'Then we'll take as many of them with us as we can.'

Drury knew the ranch was being watched even though Santiago and his bunch had — supposedly — returned to Tucson.

The man had left someone in the hills to watch the goings-on at the D Bar M spread. Grady had seen him when he was riding out to the box canyon called Friday where he was building a gate and fence across the narrow entrance, ready for the next round-up of mavericks. He thought it was the one Santiago had called Conrads but Mel Roberts claimed to have also seen the big-bellied Quick. So it looked like Santiago was shuttling his men around, using Con one day, Quick the next. There didn't seem to be any sign of Cole Fisher.

Santiago had supplied Drury with what little information he had about Montegas' plan to move Herrera from Hermosillo to Caborca. It was little enough and there was no certainty

45

about the dates for the move or even the route. The tall Mexican said he would find out more and let Drury know.

Meantime, Drury should make preparations.

'Can't do that till I know what their plans are.'

'You know you will have to get my uncle across the desert,' Santiago snapped. 'Prepare for that. Cole says you have the name for being a good tactician and strategist in the army. I suggest you see if you still possess those qualities.'

'It's easier when you have everything cut and dried for you. Going by guesswork is suicide.'

'Nevertheless, my friend, you will do as I say.'

Drury cocked his head slightly, looking at the Mexican. 'Used to getting your own way, huh?'

'You would do well to remember that, Mr Drury.'

The rancher wasn't quite sure what

the man meant until Maguire found Grady Timms lying unconscious in Friday Canyon, pinned to the ground by a small tree that had apparently toppled on him when he was felling it so as to incorporate it in the fence he was building.

He was in a bad way, with at least one leg broken and possibly his left hip. Ribs had been damaged and there was a long, deep gash running down his face from his hairline to his jaw. He had lost a good deal of blood.

Mel Roberts took him into town in the buckboard.

'Grady never felled a tree like that in his life,' Woody Maguire said, watching Drury checking his six-gun and rifle. 'He was too good an axeman.'

Drury nodded, holstering his pistol and hefting the rifle.

'Where you off to?'

'Going to see Santiago in town.'

'He'll have Cole Fisher with him.'

Drury's eyes were like chips of pale-coloured ice. 'I hope so.'

'I better come, too.'

'No, stay put, Woody. I'll be back come sundown.'

Maguire wanted to argue but Drury strode down to the corrals, roped himself a buckskin and saddled up swiftly with sure but jerky movements. Maguire sighed: he knew there was no arguing with the man when he moved like that — it meant he was boiling mad inside and sure didn't want any company . . .

Fisher wasn't with Santiago as Maguire had predicted but Conrads was and Drury thought he glimpsed Quick on the veranda of the hotel where the tall Mexican had his rooms.

He listened politely as Drury told him about Grady.

'Too bad. Still, a man unhandy with tools could be a liability on such a venture as we have planned.' The tall Mexican's dark eyes flashed at the rancher. 'You have been making your plans, I trust, Mr Drury?'

'Only broadly. I still need more

precise information. You don't seem to savvy this isn't some kind of a romp where you go in hoping to find the people you want in the place you want, and doing what you want them to. You have to *know* what they're about, know exact times and places.'

'I told you to expect to earn your money,' Santiago told him shortly. 'I am not in the charity business, Drury. I want this to work. Now you see that it does. Or perhaps another of your men may meet with an accident. Through his own clumsiness, of course.'

'You son of a bitch! I knew it was your doing, Grady being hurt like that.'

Santiago spread his arms. 'I am entirely innocent. I have been nowhere near your ranch since we met the other day.'

'How about Cole Fisher? Or Conrads here?'

Santiago shrugged. 'I do not keep them on a short rein. But you are barking up the wrong tree. Just do what I expect of you and you will have no more worries, I am sure. It's as simple as that.'

'There better not be any more 'accidents'. None at all.'

For a moment, something like fear flared briefly in the Mexican's eyes as Dave Drury set his brittle gaze on him.

'All right. Get me the information I need ... movements, times, routes planned. Meantime you and your men be ready to ride down into Mexico in a couple of nights' time.'

Santiago frowned, genuinely puzzled, 'Mexico?'

'Yeah — there's a new moon in two nights' time. Doesn't rise until almost sun-up. We call it a Rustlers' Moon — just what we want.'

'Montegas will not make his move so soon!'

'Don't expect him to. But you want us to be ready, don't you? Sure. So, have your men set for night after next, around ten. We'll meet at Apache Butte. Anyone in town'll tell you how to find it . . . '

'Wait! What are you planning . . . ?'

Drury laid a finger alongside his crooked nose and winked briefly. 'Apache Butte. Night after next. Oh, and you'd better bring your guns. With plenty of ammo.'

'Come back here, Drury! I need to know more! Come back, I say!'

Drury stepped easily into the saddle and lifted the reins. As Conrads lunged for his leg, he kicked the man in the jaw, stretching him out in the dust under the hitch rail. Drury's six-gun slid into his hand and he looked up at the veranda, hammer cocked.

'Dunno why they call you 'Quick' — I could shoot out both your eyes before you get that gun free of leather!'

The big-bellied gunman swore and lifted his hands away from his sides. Drury backed up the buckskin, wheeled and rode swiftly out of town, Santiago watching him go with narrowed eyes.

4

Rustlers' Moon

'How's Grady?' asked Maguire as Drury dismounted at the corrals in the red glow of an Arizona summer sunset.

'Doc says he'll be unconscious for a spell. Concussion, but no fracture of the skull. Busted leg and three ribs. He's gonna be laid up for a couple months.'

'Like to know where Cole Fisher was when that tree fell on Grady.'

Drury nodded and they started for the bunkhouse where the cook had supper ready.

'We'll get the straight of it, then do what we have to,' Drury said as they entered.

That was OK by Maguire and after a more or less silent meal, they went outside to sit on the bench and finish their coffee with a cigarette, watching the dying sun.

'Grady being out of it, leaves us a man short,' Drury said after a while.

'Aw, we can manage the ranch work without Grady.'

'Wasn't the ranch work I was thinking about.'

'That Herrera thing?'

Drury nodded. 'Santiago's getting impatient. Seems to expect me to have a plan all ready to go. Those two brothers who tangle with Sheriff Carlin every so often — know where they hang out?'

'Reckon I could find 'em. Mitch and Jo-Jo McLaine. That who you mean?'

'Yeah — tell 'em if they want to earn a few bucks to be down here by sundown night after tomorrow.'

'We makin' a move?'

'Kind of. We haven't paid Montez a visit in a coon's age.'

Maguire smiled slowly. 'The McLaines'll likely do it for nothin' when they know where we're goin'.'

53

'No, they'll be paid. But only if they forget their beef with Montez, and do what they're told. Make sure they savvy that, Woody. There'll be no settling old scores on this deal.'

Maguire tugged at an earlobe.

'Well, Mitch and Jo-Jo ain't exactly forgivin' folks and Montez did . . . spoil their sister.'

'They come with us, they follow orders. Any doubt about it, get someone else.'

Maguire looked sharply at Drury in the fast-fading light. 'You goin' all out on this one, then?'

'Told you, I owe Herrera. Don't like him but that makes no never mind. This is a chance to square things away.'

★   ★   ★

Apache Butte was more than half-way to the border and it blocked out a good section of stars in the night sky as Drury led his men in along the narrow trail.

There was quite a bunch of them: Drury himself, Maguire, the McLaines, Mel Roberts and a man named Howie who had roustabouted for Drury a few times in the past. When Santiago and his three hardcases joined them, there were ten riders who took the trail south towards Mexico.

'Where are we going?' snapped Santiago, ranging his big black alongside Drury's buckskin.

'Mexico.'

Santiago swore. 'You work for me, Drury! I will not be left out this way!'

Drury didn't turn his head. 'You heard of the Montez *estancia*?'

'Of course! The largest horse *rancho* in northern Mexico.'

'Right. We need fifty, sixty desert-bred horses if we're going to cross the Altar safely.'

In the faint starlight he wasn't certain if Santiago's jaw dropped briefly, but he thought so.

'I can not afford the price Montez would charge for so many *caballos*!'

'We won't be paying him anything.'

Santiago almost hauled rein, but heeled his mount forward, drawing level with the buckskin.

'You — you dare implicate *me* in — horse-rustling?'

'Figured you had a big stake in this, you'd like to be in it every step of the way.'

'You fool! Renaldo Montez has a veritable army of the finest and toughest *vaqueros* in the Americas!'

'That's his claim. But we've outwitted 'em before.' When Santiago merely stared, Drury added, 'More than half the ranches in southern Arizona are running Montez horses.'

'Then his herds will be heavily guarded.'

'Mebbe. Far as I know no one's hit him for over a year now. He'll be feeling smug and safe and he ain't a man to spend a *peso* when he don't have to. There may not be so many guards.'

'I hope I haven't made a mistake hiring you, Drury.'

The rancher smiled crookedly but he doubted that the Mexican noticed, his face being shadowed by the wide brim of his hat.

'You can call it off any time.'

Santiago said nothing for a time, then spoke quietly, the hot night breeze carrying his words clearly.

'Do not underestimate me — Lieutenant Kincaid! I still have the upper hand . . . '

* * *

They thundered on through the night and waited all next day in a brush-choked arroyo, counting Montez's riders as they moved among grazing horses that seemed to blanket the country for miles.

'He'll never miss fifty head,' Cole Fisher opined.

'We *need* fifty,' Maguire told him shortly. 'Which means we gotta grab a hundred if we can, cut out the best on the way back home.'

'While the Mexes are chasing us?' Fisher scoffed.

'They won't cross the border.'

'*We're* crossing it.'

'Yeah, but we bad *hombres*. Montez don't like *norteamericanos*. He swore a long time ago he would never set foot on American soil for any reason. Looks on it as part of Mexico that we stole a long time back. Mind, he might hire a few dozen border hardcases to recover his mustangs for him, though. But most of 'em just take his money and ride on back to the nearest cantina.'

Fisher wasn't sure whether Maguire was joshing him or not so refrained from making a comment.

The day dragged for the men but by sundown they had a better picture of where the best horses were. The *caballeros* had been cutting out bunches all day long, obviously getting them ready for market or some special job on the big estate. Montez supplied the Mexican cavalry in the northern provinces with many of their mounts.

'Them greasers are packin' plenty of hardware,' allowed Jo-Jo McLaine, a man a good eight inches shorter than his brother who was only mid-sized at best. They looked mean, though, smelled of wild trails and hard living, their clothes worn and patched. Their faces were narrow and vicious.

'And they know how to use 'em,' Mel Roberts said. 'I still got one of their slugs under my left shoulder from our last raid. Gives me hell come winter.'

'They put a slug in me,' said Mitch McLaine flatly, 'they better hope it kills me outright 'cause I'll shoot every son of a bitch in sight who rides for the Montez brand.'

'Just cut out the bunch of horses you're told to, Mitch,' Drury said flatly.

Mitch, unshaven, ugly, spat and curled a lip. Drury nodded at Maguire, telling him to keep an eye on the McLaines: it was clear they hadn't forgotten Montez had seduced their sister and turned her over to a border

brothel when he was finished with her
. . . or so they claimed.

★   ★   ★

The night was perfect for what they had
to do — and Montez had been lulled
into a false sense of security by the
apparent lack of interest shown in his
herds this last year by the Border
ranchers. The guards were scattered
and seemed lax, groups staying close to
the camp-fire, a couple riding out on
token duty every now and again to
circle the herds.

Because there was no moon, the stars
seemed more brilliant than ever. Drury
had drawn a map in the sand earlier,
showing the trails the men should take
back to the border and where they
should cross. There would be three
different groups and they would cross
at three separate places. Santiago was
impressed with Drury's knowledge of
the country and his planning. It seemed
smooth and simple.

But the McLaines nearly ruined
it . . .

* * *

Afterwards, Drury blamed himself for
not having enough sense to include the
wild brothers in the group he was
leading. Instead, he put them with
Maguire who, although a tough, reliable
man, was a mite leery of the brothers,
knowing their murderous ways.

So he sent them around one side of
the designated bunch of horses while he
took the other. The idea was for all
groups to co-ordinate their movements,
get into position and move only on
Drury's signal.

But the McLaines didn't worry about
orders. The trouble was, they recognized one of the Mexican riders as
Rodolfo, Renaldo Montez's nephew
who, border gossip-mongers claimed,
was being groomed to take over the
huge estate from the childless Montez
when the rich *ranchero* died.

Rodolfo was little more than a boy, just into his teens, yet well aware of the huge responsibility being placed upon his shoulders, determined to make his uncle proud of him.

But Mitch McLaine's rope whispered through the air and settled over the boy's slim neck, yanking him savagely out of the saddle. Sanchez, the man whose job it was to watch out for the boy, whirled his mount, clawing for his gun, but Jo-Jo shot him — and that started the horses running.

Which suited Mitch. Swearing and laughing at the same time, he pulled the rope taut and the choking boy struggled and kicked frantically as he was dragged through the dust. There were shouts and more shots and the horses thundered forward, whinnying, rolling their eyes.

Rodolfo gave a choked scream that was lost in the general din as Mitch pulled him right into the path of the stampeding horses — then dropped the suddenly slack rope.

The other selected bunches were also on the move but not in any way that would allow them to be controlled by Drury's men as he had planned. This was out-and-out stampede, panic communicating itself to all the horses as they surged forward and wheeled and weaved this way and that, shrilling and whinnying as they rolled bulging eyes.

Guns thundered and men toppled from their saddles. Mitch yelled in triumph:

'Tell Montez he can have what's left of his kid with the compliments of the McLaines.'

Jo-Jo cut loose with a war whoop and triggered into the air. He should have directed his bullets to the two Mexican riders cutting between him and his brother. They caught him in a crossfire and his small body jerked and shuddered before spilling from the saddle.

Mitch McLaine called his brother's name, rode in on the Mexicans, six-gun roaring, cutting one down, the other swaying in the saddle as he veered away.

McLaine rode after him, weaving his mount by knee-pressure between the running horses, and reached out with his smoking Colt, rammed it against the Mexican's head and dropped hammer. As the man was blown out of the saddle, McLaine wrenched his reins and fought his way into the midst of the running horses, crouching low in the saddle, making himself an almost impossible target.

Thick dust blanketed the night, blotting out the stars which Drury had aimed to use for direction so as to get the horses back to the border. He spat grit and rubbed at his stinging eyes with his shirt-sleeve, trying to clear his vision, cursing Mitch McLaine and his long-standing hatred for Montez.

There were hundreds of mounts running wild now and the Mexicans had given up trying to kill the rustlers, doing what they could to cut out bunches from the huge group that was consolidating down in the dry washes, aiming to save as many of the horses for

Montez as they could.

Howie's riderless horse was running with the stampede now, stirrups banging, caught up in the rush. Mel was nursing a wounded arm, trying to tie a neckerchief about it, using his teeth to draw the knot tight. Maguire's head was humming: a slug had torn off his hat and grazed his skull, cutting a furrow through his hair. He felt disoriented and only Drury's hand on his reins guided his mount to safety.

Santiago's group seemed to have done best of all, cutting out more than seventy horses and were now already on the trail back to the part of the border Drury had assigned to them.

Now that the horses were once again scattering as they surged up out of the washes and arroyos on to flat country, the Mexicans were peeling off and coming after the *norteamericano* robbers. A racket of shots brought fresh whinnies of panic from the horses and some that had been settling into a long-striding, controlled run, suddenly reared and shrilled and began to break away. Gunflashes stabbed the night from both sides. Drury's rifle jarred his shoulder as he shot down two Mexican mounts, the riders being thrown heavily.

Some of the Mexicans, wise to the ways of past American rustlers, rode on ahead and tried to ambush them at the border crossings. But Drury had changed the usual places, only by a few hundred yards, enough so that they had most of the horses across before the Mexicans came riding in, red-faced and shooting.

But, once the horses were on the US side, the Mexicans fell back although they fired plenty of shots — and plenty answered them.

★   ★   ★

Two hours past midnight and the dishevelled, bloody, dust-spattered rustlers met at the rendezvous; a quick head-count told Drury they had more than a hundred horses, about a hundred and twenty-seven, he reckoned.

Plenty to allow them to pick fifty or sixty of the best. The remainder he would drive back across the border as he usually did. He never knew how Montez regarded this . . .

Satisfied with the way it had turned out after all, he went looking for Mitch McLaine.

'Rode out, Dave,' Maguire told him, holding a wet cloth to the wound in his scalp. 'Said you can keep the money: he's been paid for tonight's work.'

'You were a fool to hire him in the first place,' said Santiago sourly, dusting himself down. 'The man has jeopardized the whole deal.'

'We've got the horses we want,' Drury told him.

'You really believe a man like Montez will not cross the border now? After your man killed his nephew? You are a bigger fool than I thought.'

Drury turned back to Maguire. 'Which way'd he go, Woody?'

'Makin' for Nogales, I'd reckon. He kept a woman there.'

Drury changed horses, throwing his saddle on to a big grey gelding and turning the sweating buckskin loose.

'Be back by sun-up,' he told Maguire. 'Cut out the best and get 'em moving out towards the spread. I'll catch up.'

'Watch your back!' Maguire called after him. 'Mitch don't often see the face of a man he aims to kill!'

* * *

The shot crashed and reverberated through the rocks, slapped back from the stone walls of the canyon, but before the bullet ricocheted from the high boulder near his shoulder, Drury was diving out of the saddle, snatching his rifle as he went.

He hit the ground rolling and two more shots kicked gravel into his face. He ducked his head and stones rattled against the stiff brim of his hat as he spun around behind a low rock, lever working on the Winchester. He saw the gunsmoke spurting from the high rocks half-way to the rim of the canyon, placed his first shot in amongst those same rocks. He heard the buzz of the ricochet and, hard on its heels, the startled grunt from Mitch McLaine.

The bushwhacker stood, rifle coming to his shoulder. There was blood streaking one side of his face as he pumped several shots at Drury's rock before his gun went silent. Dave Drury was on his feet instantly, running, weaving as the man hastily reloaded. He glimpsed Mitch's white face as the man looked up to see how close Drury was, saw the killer drop a shell and frantically shuck another from his belt.

Drury's long legs were pounding hard and he hit the slope with a leap, driving himself up, teeth bared with effort. He swung his rifle in front and got off three fast shots that sent rock-chips and dust spurting over Mitch. The man swore, made to weave to one side, lost his footing and fell.

Drury's next shot was a lucky one and it jarred the rifle from McLaine's hand.

Cursing, still sliding on the slope, McLaine rolled on to his back, groping for his six-gun. He got it free but he was too close to Drury by then and the rancher struck it from his hand with his rifle barrel. Mitch scrambled in an effort to get to his feet, flinging a handful of gravel.

Drury jerked his head aside, slammed the rifle across Mitch's ribs. The man grunted and staggered, grabbing at his side. He ducked his head and charged at Drury, arms reaching for the rancher's body. Drury stepped nimbly aside, smashed his rifle barrel across McLaine's back. The man's breath exploded from him and he sprawled face down. As he made to get up, gagging, Drury kicked him in the head.

He leaned down, grabbed the dazed man's shirt and hurled him back violently against a boulder. The breath slammed out of Mitch and he sat there, eyes glazing, face bloody, looking up, awaiting his fate.

'C'mon, Mitch — there's a man waiting to see you.'

Drury dragged him down the slope by his shirt and flung him against a rock at the bottom. He took his rope from the saddle horn of the grey and stooped over McLaine, twisting him onto his face and lashing his wrists behind him.

'Next time you'll do what you're told,' Drury said, picking up the coiled rope. 'Only there ain't gonna be a next time for you, Mitch, old pard. My guess is you've come to the end of your trail and I can't think of anyone who'll be sorry to learn that, you murdering son of a bitch!'

He mounted the grey, shouldering aside Mitch roughly, paying out a couple of yards of rope. He yanked hard and McLaine stumbled, righted himself, then staggered along behind Drury's mount as they headed back towards the border.

5

Fair Exchange

It was full daylight by the time they reached the border and the dust of the stolen herd was only a smudge on the horizon to the north-west.

Maguire had apparently done a good, fast job of sorting out the horses and when Drury looked across the shallow trench-like line that roughly marked the border between Arizona and Mexico, he could see scattered horses over on the Mexican side, grazing.

He also saw something else: a heavy dust-cloud, approaching from the south over there, with a tight, though moving black line beneath it. Thumbing back his hat and wiping a forearm across his dusty, sweat-streaked face, Drury looked down at Mitch McLaine. The man was sprawled in the coarse sand, still gasping from the run he had been forced to make at the end of the rope. He turned a grey, drawn, dirt-smudged face up to the rancher.

'You're a dead man, Drury!' he gasped, voice hoarse and raspy.

Drury nodded to the dust cloud over in Mexico. 'Not if who I think is riding with that bunch, Mitch . . . '

He yanked on the rope and put the horse forward, forcing McLaine up on to his feet. Swearing, Mitch staggered after the grey to a stand of trees. Drury dismounted, kicked Mitch in the back of the legs so that the man dropped to his knees, and cut the rope, leaving the wrists still bound. The rancher swiftly made a sliding knot and a loop, dropped the loop over the startled McLaine's neck.

'The hell's goin' on?' Mitch demanded, voice echoing the fear that suddenly surged through him.

Drury said nothing until he had the free end of the rope tossed over a branch. Then he hauled it taut and tugged until McLaine staggered awkwardly to his feet.

'Wait up, dammit! You can't — '

'Stand up on the rock, Mitch,' Drury ordered.

McLaine stared. 'No! Look, you can't string me up . . . ' His words faded to a strangled growl as Drury hauled on the rope and whether he wanted to or not, the only way Mitch could ease the pressure stretching his neck was for him to step up on to the low rock, about two and a half feet high. He swayed awkwardly on top of the rock and the slack in the rope was swiftly taken up.

Drury tied it around the trunk of the tree. 'Better stand mighty still, Mitch. You fall now and you'll swing. No way your feet can reach the ground.'

'Aw, come on, Drury! We never been friends but there ain't no need for this!'

Drury rolled and lit a cigarette, took a long draw and then placed it between McLaine's suddenly dry lips.

'Enjoy it, Mitch. It's likely your last.'

'What you gonna do?'

'Not up to me.' Drury indicated the large bunch of riders coming in, now clearly visible. There were about twenty men, all wearing distinctive sombreros.

Mitch frowned, turning his head a little to avoid the smoke curling up from the cigarette.

'You turnin' me over to them?' His words were barely audible.

Drury said nothing, poured some water from his canteen into his hat and gave it to the grey horse. He swigged some himself and settled down in the shade, ignoring the stream of curses that Mitch McLaine threw his way.

In ten minutes the band of Mexicans were lined up along their side of the border. There was a man in the centre of the line, riding a glistening black Arab, his saddle ornate with inlaid silver and with a high back. Beneath the sombrero some steel-grey hair showed and the shadowed face was dark and wolfish. Either side of him sat hard-eyed men holding rifles with the butts resting on their thighs.

'So. You replenish your herds from my horses once again, Drury!' said the man on the Arab.

'It was necessary, Señor Montez . . . I have kept fifty. The raid was meant to be bloodless.'

Montez's black, burning eyes swivelled to McLaine.

'You mean to hang that man?'

'I could — but it's up to you.'

'Ah! So this is the one who killed Rodolfo?'

'He's the one, Señor Montez. It should never have happened. I blame myself, but I can't bring your nephew back. Giving you his killer is as close as I can come to some kind of atonement.'

Montez was silent a long time, staring at McLaine who swallowed, then spat out the cigarette that had burned down now.

'Do your worst, greaser! I told you a long time back I'd square with you one day for what you done to my sister.'

Montez still didn't answer for

another long minute.

'You are mistaken. I did nothing to your sister. It is a long story and serves no purpose now to tell it except to say she is living a life of luxury in Mexico City and has never been happier since running away from you and your murderous brother.' He flicked his gaze to Drury as McLaine ranted, calling him a liar. 'You are still a smart man, Drury. You think by turning this scum over to me, it will prevent me sending men after your rustlers . . . ?'

'I'd hoped it'd work out that way. This is important, Señor Montez. It involves an old friend of yours — Carlos Herrera.'

Montez stiffened slightly, frowning.

'The General? How is this? Come over here and tell me, Drury. I grow hoarse shouting.' He turned to the rifleman on his left and the man threw the weapon to his shoulder and fired. The rope coiled down around McLaine's shoulders, startling him so that he overbalanced and fell off the rock to sprawl on the ground.

By the time he had managed to stumble to his feet, two Mexicans were beside him, grabbing his arms, dragging him back across the border trench to stand before Montez on his Arab. McLaine was still defiant, curled his lip at the ageing *ranchero*.

'I look forward to spending a lot of time with you, *señor*,' Montez said heavily and something in his voice and face made McLaine suddenly go pale and silent.

He was led away and roughly roped to the saddle of one of the Mexicans. The rope was short and Drury knew the man would be dragged off his feet before the rider had gone more than a few yards. But he felt no sympathy for McLaine; he turned to face Montez.

'What is to stop me having you roped to another of my men's saddles, Drury? You have helped yourself to my herds for years — I could show you my displeasure.'

'Your honour wouldn't let you, Señor

Montez. I have given you the man you really want and I am about to offer to pay you for the fifty horses my men are driving back to my ranch. But I cannot do this until I receive payment from a man called Santiago who wants me to help set Herrera free.'

Montez showed real interest now.

'Then let us find some shade and you can tell me more about this . . . '

★   ★   ★

Jason Santiago's face was straight and taut as he looked at Drury sitting his dusted grey, hands folded on the saddle horn.

'Montez! You told him about our mission?'

'He's an old friend of the general, has been trying for a long time to find out what's really happened to him. Now he knows where he's being held, he says he can soon learn the details of the move from Hermosillo.'

Santiago's dark eyes narrowed. 'And

he, no doubt, will want to join us and grab his share of the glory.'

'He says he can let us have some men if we need them. He's not looking for glory. Just wants his old friend to have a chance . . . which he don't have with Montegas. They keep shifting him about so no one knows for sure where he is. Eventually he'll be killed but everything will be so mixed up no one'll know exactly what happened. Or where. I think Montez means well. And we can do with some help.'

'He let you go, at least!' There was suspicion in the Mexican's tone.

'He has my word I'll pay for the horses and I handed him the man who killed his nephew. That kind of wiped my slate clean with Montez.'

Santiago still looked sceptical.

'I don't like outsiders being brought into my plans without consultation.'

Drury straightened in the saddle and gestured behind him.

'You ride hard, you'll catch him before he gets back to his *rancho*. You can tell him to forget it, if you want.'

'I warned you once, Drury! Do — not — push — me!'

The rancher smiled crookedly. 'You keep reminding me that you can blackmail me because of my past, Santiago. Here's something for you to chew on: you *need* me if you're going to get Herrera across that desert. There's not another white man living who can do it. You want to think about that?'

Santiago didn't like that and his nostrils pinched, took on a white-rimmed look as he fought to control his temper.

'Very well. But there will be an accounting, Drury, make no mistake.'

Drury nodded, still half smiling. 'That's the part I'm looking forward to.'

He wheeled the grey and rode in the direction of the horses that Maguire and the others were driving hard towards the distant D Bar M.

Santiago looked around him a little wildly, then climbed into his saddle and took out his rage on his mount, raking savagely with his large rowels. He lashed and spurred the big mount towards Cole Fisher who was riding drag on the southern fringe of the stolen horses.

* * *

After supper back at the ranch most of the men who had ridden to Mexico turned in early. Drury and Maguire smoked their usual after-supper ciga-rettes on the bench outside the bunkhouse, watching the sundown fire paint the sky.

'Montez goin' to come through, you reckon?' asked Maguire.

'Think he will, Woody. My stock's gone up with him since I turned McLaine over.'

Maguire looked uncomfortable in the ruddy light. 'Felt bad about that, Dave.'

'You couldn't know the kid would be there and that the McLaines would do what they did. I sure wouldn't want to be Mitch McLaine right now.'

'No. Some of the things we've heard about what Montez does to fellers who steal his broncs make a man shudder. Hate to think what he'll do to the man who killed his only heir . . . '

'I thought of killing Mitch myself, but knew the only way to keep Montez off our tails was to give him his nephew's murderer. Don't set all that easy, Woody.'

'It worked. I guess that's the main thing.' Maguire flicked away his cigarette, stood and ground it out under his boot and hitched at his gun belt. 'I'm turnin' in. Gonna relieve Mel round about midnight.'

Drury stifled a yawn. 'The horses have settled fairly well. Might be 'cause they're tired after the drive, but if they stay quiet, turn in. The corrals'll hold 'em and I don't think they'll fuss before sun-up.'

Drury lost no time in hitting the hay himself.

★ ★ ★

Woody Maguire was still heavy with sleep when he relieved Mel at the far side of the big holding corrals.

'How they been?'

'Not bad.' Mel, too, yawned. 'A few a little skittish but reckon they'll settle down completely before long. Man, the thought of that bunk sure makes me feel good! *Buenos noches*, Woody . . . '

Maguire watched Mel ride up towards the ranch until he disappeared from sight, then he rode round the corrals. A few of the horses kicked at the rails in protest, used to running free on the wide plains of Mexico, but they were too weary to put much effort into it. Maguire spoke to them softly, even tried an off-key song or two, found himself dozing in the saddle.

The temptation to just ride on back to the bunkhouse was strong, but he figured he would stay at least an hour, make sure the broncs weren't suddenly going to wake up after a short sleep and be fiery and foul-tempered. He'd seen more than one bunch of half-wild broncs reduce a corral to a pile of matchwood overnight . . .

Despite himself he dozed in the saddle — and awoke with a jerk as a rope settled over his upper body, pinning his arms. He started to yell and was yanked violently off his mount which whinnied and shied away. Maguire hit the ground hard, grunting, fighting for breath as he rolled, trying to get his legs under him.

A shadow moved across the stars, towering over him. He thought he saw the pale, brief flash of teeth as the man grinned. Then the first boot drove into his ribs and brought a strangled cry of pain from him. The second boot slammed against the side of his head and it felt like it had been torn off his shoulders.

But only briefly, before he fell into the fireworks that exploded behind his eyes and more red pain shook his body . . .

There was a period of blackness and

then the ordeal of regaining consciousness to find he was roped to a tree. A
gloved hand twisted in his hair, yanked
his head up, rapping his skull against
the tree-trunk, and then another gloved
fist smashed him in the middle of the
face. He felt his nose go, blood gushing.

Those same fists hammered his face
until he couldn't see out of swollen,
torn eyes. Then they moved to his body
and expertly hammered his ribs and
midriff, never hard enough to make
him lose consciousness, but plenty hard
enough to hurt like hell. He heard the
grunts of effort of his attacker, thought
there were others standing to one side
but couldn't be sure. *Waiting their
turn? Hell, he hoped not!*

A knee drove up between his legs and
he gagged sickly, the ropes keeping
him from doubling over. The blows
increased in pace and force, the
hammering tattoo rocking his body
without cease. And, *he thought he
heard his assailant singing to himself!*
At least humming in time with the

blows as they drove home in a crippling rhythm. But consciousness was fast slipping away from Maguire and his legs buckled so that his body hung limply against the ropes.

And still the fists continued to hammer home, the dark attacker dancing from side to side of his victim, fists darting, the rough leather gloves twisting with each blow as it landed so as to cause the most pain and damage.

Through the haze of pain and dizziness Maguire thought, *the sonuver knows what he's doing! He's not crippling me, just making it hurt like hell!*

Then he passed out and even then the beating continued for a few minutes more. At least he didn't feel that part.

But when he came round it would be a different story.

★   ★   ★

It was Drury who found him just on first light.

The rancher had wakened early and figured to go see how the horses had settled in, for they would have to be broken to the saddle a little more before they could be put to use. He walked down from the house, rolling his first cigarette of the day, lit up and was flicking away the used match when he saw the huddled body at the foot of a tree.

He sprinted across, dropped to one knee, recognizing Maguire's clothes even though they were torn and bloody. He quickly examined the man, ran back to the bunkhouse, poked his head in the door and yelled for Mel, not caring if he woke Santiago and his men in the nearby barn. He signalled for Cookie to come with him, ordering the man to bring a dish of hot water and some rags.

Maguire was not a pretty sight with the gravel sticking to the blood and torn skin of his face and he didn't look much better even after the cook had washed him with hands gentle as a woman's. By that time, Mel had arrived, also Con Conrads and Cole Fisher. Quick lounged in the big doorway of the barn but there was no sign of Santiago.

'Who done it, Dave?' asked Mel as he helped Cookie smear salves over Maguire's wounds. The man was still out to it though breathing steadily enough. Both eyes were swollen and blackened, his nose enlarged and puffed, nostrils crusted with dried blood. He had lost two teeth and a deal of skin from his body where boots had torn through his shirt before peeling off flesh.

'Some beating,' Cole allowed, rolling a cigarette.

Drury stood, looking steadily at the man. 'Those new work gloves?' he asked as he saw Fisher awkwardly trying to smoothe his cigarette paper into a cylinder.

'Tolerably. Been wearing 'em for a few days.'

Drury didn't believe the man but said nothing. Cookie gathered all the bloody rags and Maguire's torn shirt and walked down past the outhouse to dump them in the garbage pit. Santiago appeared, running a comb through wet hair, adjusting his shirt. He took the scene in briefly and shook his head slowly.

'You must be jinxed, Drury — all your men seem to be having — accidents.'

'This was no accident,' Drury told him sharply. 'Funny thing, every time I have words with you, something happens to one of my men.'

Santiago shrugged. 'Like I said — jinxed.'

'Dave!'

The rancher turned at the urgent cry from Cookie, saw the man standing by the outhouse, gesturing for Drury to join him. The group frowned as he walked across with long strides and Cookie led him around the rear of the outhouse.

The old man pointed down into the garbage pit. Lying on top of the food scraps and rubbish were a pair of torn leather work gloves, half-curled from long use and stained darkly.

Drury slid down the steep slope, grabbed the nearest one and tossed it up to the cook while he climbed out. Cookie whistled.

'That's bloodstains! And still damp!'

Drury said nothing, took the glove, heeled smartly and strode back towards the waiting group, Mel kneeling now with Maguire's head in his lap as the man started to come round slowly. Santiago and his men had been joined by Quick and all four watched Drury warily as he approached.

He didn't stop.

Instead of pausing a few feet in front of them as would be expected, Drury walked right up to the startled Cole Fisher and lashed him brutally, back and forth across the face with the recovered glove.

Fisher staggered and Drury threw away the blood-stained glove, grabbed Cole's right arm and ran him head first into the top pole of the corral. He shoved the dazed man's hand through the bars, twisted the forearm up and over so he could examine the new glove — and then he ripped it off, revealing the bruised and torn flesh underneath where the old glove had ripped and offered no protection.

Drury's elbow rammed backwards as Fisher struggled to get free and it smashed savagely between Fisher's eyes. His head snapped back; Drury released his hold and the man sat down heavily in the gravel. Drury placed a boot in the middle of the man's chest and pinned him to the ground, his face cold and murderous.

'There are rope marks on Maguire's arms and rubbings on the tree, which means you tied him up and then worked him over. You ain't lost your touch since the army, Cole. Knew just how hard to hit him and where, didn't you? Make him hurt, make him feel it for a few days or a week, but not enough to stop him working ... You yeller-bellied snake!'

Drury's boot took Cole Fisher under the jaw, the man's teeth clacking together loudly. His head jerked to one side and he grunted as he rolled away. He drew his knees up and with head hanging, spat bloody saliva into the dirt. Then he turned his head slowly and glared hotly up at Dave Drury.

'You bastard! You ain't changed, either! Still think you're tough, don't you?'

Drury spread his hands. 'I'm not tied to a tree.'

Cole Fisher growled deep in his throat and suddenly launched himself at Drury's legs. The rancher was a mite slow in back-pedalling and Cole managed to get one arm wrapped around. Drury staggered and while trying to regain his balance, Fisher hooked a leg out from under him, thrusting upwards. Drury fell on his back and Fisher bared broken, bloodstained teeth as he flung himself bodily on to the man. But like a flash, Drury pulled his knees up and they caught Fisher in the midriff. They didn't hurt him much but they took his wind for a second and he rolled to one side.

By then, Dave Drury was on his feet and Cole came up roaring and swinging. Drury stepped swiftly aside, spun around and hooked a left against the side of the man's shaggy head. Cole stumbled to one knee, hands reaching out for Drury so as to steady himself. The rancher contemptuously knocked them aside, lifted a knee into Cole's face. The man went over backwards, but this time he continued the movement, somersaulting, coming up fast and launching himself forward like a human battering-ram.

It took Drury by surprise and the thick arms encircled his waist as Fisher's head rammed into his belly and the man's sheer weight carried him over backwards. Cole pulled away as Drury was falling and was balanced for a kick when the rancher struck the ground. He grinned as he drove his boot into Drury's side, bringing a loud, involuntary grunt from the rancher.

Drury sprawled and Fisher laughed as he strode in stomping. A boot-heel caught Drury's shoulder, ripping his shirt and the flesh underneath. Dave's arm went numb and he rolled on to that side, keeping it close to his body, using his right arm to thrust away and roll into a rising position. Fisher, the old army brawler who had learned his fighting in the camps of the mountain men along the Yellowstone many years ago, crouched low, suddenly leaped to one side and behind Drury, catching him unawares. A fist like a hammer slammed into the back of Drury's head and drove him down, face first into the gravel. He instinctively rolled on to his back to meet the attack that he knew would come from above, hands rising and crossing protectively before his face.

He caught Cole Fisher's boot as it drove brutally towards his face, strained to keep it from crushing his nose and with a grunting heave, twisted and lifted his upper body against the downward pressure. Fisher was balanced only on one leg and he stumbled. Dave pushed harder, rose higher, got a leg under him, thrust with that, then with both legs. He threw Cole Fisher ten feet, the man's leg rising violently above his head, tearing the groin muscles so that Fisher yelled and writhed when he hit the ground, grabbing at his strained leg.

Dave Drury blotted sweat from his face with the torn sleeve of his shirt and stumbled across. He bared his teeth as he reached down for what was left of the front of Fisher's shirt, hauled him unceremoniously to his feet, then head-butted him in the middle of the face.

Every man there heard Fisher's nose go and the blood sprayed red in the early sunlight. Cole staggered but Dave didn't release his hold on the shirt. With his right fist clubbed, he hammered it into Fisher's blood-spattered face three times, each time driving downwards as if pounding in a six-inch nail. Cole was on his knees, eyes rolling in their sockets, arms hanging limply, jaw slack and drooling blood and spittle.

Dave, breathing hard, looked down at him, curled a lip, then with a snarl of disdain flung the man from him like a bag of garbage. Cole sprawled in the dust on his face and lay still except for his heaving chest.

'Dave!' called Mel warningly and Drury spun, hand instinctively dropping to his gun as he saw Quick snatching at his own weapon.

Drury's gun came up smoothly and shattered the early morning with its roar. Quick staggered, snatching at his forearm, his gun spinning away, catching sunlight briefly before skidding in the dust. The big-bellied man sobbed and blood oozed between his fingers.

'We need you to help work the horses — otherwise you'd be dead!' Dave told him, the words coming hard and breathless. He looked at Con Conrads who lifted both hands away from his gun, well out to the side. Then Drury set his gaze on Jason Santiago and moved towards him.

The tall Mexican took a rapid step backward, lifting a hand. 'Now, wait up, Drury! You kill me and your true identity goes to the army! I wasn't fooling about the paper my attorney has!'

Dave stopped, contempt and hatred mixing on his battered face, narrowing his eyes so they looked like chips of ice.

'A slip, Santiago! *My* attorney, you said. Be no trouble to find out who that is and go see him, take the paper away from him . . .'

Santiago blanched, realizing his mistake. He forced a tight grin.

'We — we can still work together, Dave! There's that five thousand I promised you — and — well, there could be a lot more . . . All right, I shouldn't have turned Cole loose on your men. I just wanted to remind you who was running things here, but

. . . why don't we set aside our differences and really get working on this? It'll be worth your while, I promise you.'

'You really think I'd trust you now?'

Santiago shrugged. 'When it is to our mutual benefit, why not . . . ?'

'I can think of plenty of reasons, but for now I'll say this: the next time one of your men beats up on one of mine, I'll kill him. And you, too. Then I'll go find your attorney before he has time to send word to the army. Savvy?'

Santiago's dark gaze slitted but he nodded slowly, his purplish lips rimmed with white beneath the neat moustache, a pale, yellowish tinge to his swarthy skin.

No man had ever been able to put raw fear into his belly and keep it burning there like this Drury. No man.

It was a feeling Santiago did not like.

6

Pistoleros

Something had happened to Woody Maguire during that beating.

Not just the obvious injuries, but something on the inside. He had always been a happy-go-lucky kind of cowboy, always willing to lend a hand with work or helping home a fellow ranch hand who had too much redeye under his belt, or even lending the occasional dollar. He enjoyed a joke, both practical and the story kind, was always ready to grin or laugh.

But after he came round from that night's beating and saw the battered state of Cole Fisher, his bruised and cut face straightened out and his smile disappeared — not that he had been smiling when he had come back to his senses, but there was no evidence of it afterwards when a man might expect to see at least a hint of it.

'You still hurting. Woody?' Drury asked as they sat on the porch smoking and watching the sun slide down into the hills as they had done most nights over the past six years.

'I'll get over it,' Maguire said curtly and that brought Drury's head around with a snap.

'You need a sawbones?'

'Hell, *no*, I don't need no damn sawbones! Fisher knew his job too well to cripple me up. I'm achin' from scalp to toenails and in between feels like a hoss stomped me, but I can still do my chores.'

'You sound like something's bothering you.'

Maguire held the rancher's steady gaze in the ruddy, dying light. 'It bothers me how easy that son of a bitch turned me into a piece of raw meat! Never even spoke, just walked right up and started beatin' the hell outta me and I took it!'

'Christ, Woody, there were *three* of them, two holding you before they tied you to that tree. No man could've done much in those circumstances.'

'I dunno about anyone else, all I know is I din' even get in one single lick! I just got worked over any which way he felt like . . . and it don't set easy, Dave.'

'Hell, forget it, Woody! Fisher's had his lesson and he's smart enough to learn by it.'

Maguire was silent for a long moment. 'And that's another thing that don't set easy — you beatin' up on Fisher. Like I couldn't handle it!'

This was a new Woody Maguire. Dave Drury had never seen him like this before.

'Hell, Cole needed a beating, has needed one for years. If it'd been any other of the men, Mel, Grady, Cookie, I'd've done the same. Look at you now, Woody. You couldn't take on Cole Fisher without risking a real crippling-up. You'd be waiting a few weeks before you'd feel fit enough to tackle the son of a bitch and he needed that beating right then and there — before things got outta hand and Santiago got the notion he could run things any way he wanted. Ain't no reflection on you or your backbone. It was pure pleasure hammering that snake into the ground.'

'For you! Like you was a father workin' over the school bully.'

'Judas, Woody, what the hell's the matter with you? This ain't like you at all.'

Maguire flung down his cigarette and ground it savagely into the ground. He stood, hitching at his belt. He sighed.

'Well, I dunno, Dave — it's just the way I feel right now. I've never had me a beatin' just like that and I guess it makes me feel kinda — useless.'

'The hell with that. I'm about to give you the most important part of this set-up right now, aimed to before we finished supper tonight.'

Maguire looked suspicious. 'Yeah? What's that? Checkin' the ridin' gear?'

Drury smiled crookedly, shaking his head. He took a square of folded paper from his shirt pocket, opened it out. It was a rough map drawn in pencil. The rancher handed it to Maguire who frowned hard at it, turning the paper to catch the fading light.

'Nothin' more'n a few squiggly lines and blobs.'

'They're landmarks, but I'll *tell* you what to look for so if anyone else gets hold of the map they still won't know where it's leading. It's the Altar, Woody.'

Maguire whistled softly as he lifted his head. 'Never knew there was *any* kinda map of that damn desert.'

'It's as I recall it, the way Crooked Tree showed me. This is the trail down from the border, running south-east, with a sharp bend towards dead south. These 'blobs' are landmarks I'll tell you about. Near each is a sunken canyon with grass for mebbe a dozen horses. Kind of like a miniature Palo Duro on the Texas Panhandle. We've got plenty of broncs. We'll leave 'em at those places, ten in each — that's more'n we need, but you have to have all kinds of back-up in a desert like the Altar.'

'If there's grass, there's water, right?'

'Not necessarily. Underground, sure, but a long way under, yet a kind of stunted grass will still grow. Any water we need will have to be packed in.'

Maguire gave one of his low whistles. 'Man, that's some operation!'

'And I'm putting you in charge of it, Woody. You know a little about that desert but you follow this here map and find the landmarks I tell you about and we'll be able to get Herrera across to the Gulf and the boat that's s'posed to be waiting.'

Maguire blew out his cheeks, for the moment, anyway, having apparently pushed his feelings of inadequacy to the back of his mind.

'I'll need a team of good men — and burros.'

'We'll get 'em. Santiago can foot the bill, but you're the one gonna have to lead 'em in there and set up the escape route. Now I know you can do it, Woody. How d'*you* feel about it?'

Maguire looked up and in the last of the sundown light, Drury saw with relief that the old devil-may-care look was starting to appear again.

'You bust them broncs and they'll be waitin' for you, Dave. And, listen — thanks for beatin' Fisher's head in. Sorry for all the bitchin' . . . I was feelin' kind of a misery.' He rubbed at his midriff. 'By God, I hurt in here! But thanks to you, Fisher'll be hurtin', too!'

Drury grinned as they shook.

'Pleasure, Woody. Pure, unadulterated pleasure!'

★   ★   ★

The horses weren't as hard to break in as Drury had first thought. They were the offspring of animals that Montez had been breeding for years and had a kind of built-in affinity for saddle-work pulsing through their blood.

Not that they didn't have spirit — Drury's aching tail-bone was proof that they still had plenty of buck and jump in their wiry bodies. He worked hard and Cole Fisher and Santiago's men pitched in with Mel and Maguire. The tall Mexican tended to stand to one side and watch, smoking his cigarillos. Fisher hadn't said much since the fight but occasionally Drury caught him watching him with narrowed eyes that were filled with hate.

The large fenced pasture where they put the horses that were saddle-broken gradually began to fill up and it was getting close to the thirty mark when Maguire whistled from the top rail of the fence. Drury was preparing his saddle for the next bronc to be busted, looked up, saw his pard standing on the rails, pointing.

A rolling cloud of dust approached slowly, coming in from the south-west. There were black dots bobbing up and down and occasionally disappearing into the reddish haze. Riders.

And they were all wearing big hats . . .

'Mexes!' said Cole Fisher and immediately drew his six-gun, started checking the loads.

'Take it easy,' Drury said. 'It's not big enough for a raiding party and Montez wouldn't send in a bunch as small as that anyway if he wanted our scalps.'

Fisher ignored Drury, went to where his saddle was draped over the top rail of the small corral and slid his rifle out of the scabbard. Conrads and Quick did the same. Santiago, who had been resting on the porch, was on his feet now, staring at the approaching dust-cloud.

Maguire came and stood beside Mel and Drury.

'First time I've seen Mexes in a bunch comin' this far north.'

Drury nodded, squinting as the riders drew closer.

'I make it eight. One of 'em's wearing a smaller hat, looks like a kid.'

'Or a gal,' Mel said: he had good

eyesight. He grinned quickly, ran a tongue around the inside of his lower lip. 'We don't get many fee-male visitors, Dave. You been holdin' out on us?'

Drury didn't answer, watched Santiago's men line up with rifles at the ready, spread out in a line. Maybe they had the right idea but a hunch told him these riders weren't threatening. Anyway, they'd be in the yard in ten minutes and then everyone would know what was going on . . .

Mel was right: the rider in the small hat was a woman. Or a girl — she was pretty young, Drury thought, although there was a maturity in her face at the same time. Someone who had been around? Or someone who had seen the darker side of life from a wider perspective? Either way, she was the kind of girl-woman that would get plenty of looks from the men — and plenty from the women, too, though these would not be the same as the men's.

She sat easily astride a slim-legged silver-grey mare that had a roll to its eyes that Drury was damn sure he wouldn't trust. But maybe it trusted the rider and she would have no such trouble. He had miscounted, too: there were nine men and the girl. She edged her mare forward, tossing her head a little, the raven-black hair glistening as it caught sunlight and settled again about her shoulders. Her clothes were dusty but of good quality; a plain silk blouse with frilly cuffs, a yellow cummerbund around a slim waist, and a brown skirt that didn't quite cover the tooled-leather riding-boots or the silver spurs attached to them.

'I am Consuela de la Vega, ward of Don Renaldo Montez. He sends me to you with his greetings and these men if you wish to use them.' She gestured vaguely to the bunch of dusty riders who were watching Cole Fisher and his sidekicks warily. 'I am speaking with Señor Drury?'

'Yeah, I'm Drury, señorita. Good of

Señor Montez to send us the men. I can use them for sure. But — well, I don't think I have a lot of use for a girl right now, no offence intended, ma'am.'

She did not smile and the sober expression did not change. The mare moved restlessly and she tugged the reins, automatically, quieting it easily.

'I am here to deliver news to you about General Herrera. But I am sure you can — use — me beyond that. It is something we will discuss inside.'

Used to giving orders, thought Drury as Consuela dismounted and gestured towards the house. Drury shrugged and walked alongside her. Santiago fell in on the other side and she looked at him, then at Drury. The rancher made the introductions and the girl stopped.

'I have no instructions about you, Señor Santiago. I have heard of you but my message from Don Renaldo is for Señor Drury only.'

'Well, you haven't got the full picture, *señorita,*' smiled Santiago. 'Drury works

111

for me and I am interested in all news of Herrera.'

'Nonetheless, I was told to speak with Señor Drury and no one else,' she said firmly. 'It is up to him whether he tells you what I have to say.'

Santiago's dark face coloured and he started to speak, but the girl took Drury's arm impatiently and moved on towards the house. The tall Mexican frowned, made as if to follow, then changed his mind, stood there, fumbling for a fresh cigarillo, an ugly twist to his mouth.

More and more he felt that he was losing control of this situation, and it was a feeling he didn't like. At all . . .

Inside the house, the girl accepted a cup of cool water from the terracotta jug that stood in the breeze near the rear door. As he was setting the jug down, Drury saw Cole Fisher casually limping by, still suffering from the beating he had taken at the rancher's hands. He scowled as Drury deliberately closed the door, dropped the bar

112

across and then went back to where the girl waited in the parlour.

She had some papers spread out on the cluttered desk, having pushed Drury's untidy piles of ranch books to one side.

'The general will be moved in three weeks' time from Hermosillo to Caborca,' she said without preamble, pointing to a map that had a wavy line marked in red, linking the two towns. 'This is the route they will take although Don Renaldo said to tell you that it could be changed. However, he has agents who will advise him of any last-minute adjustments to the arrangements. There will be a heavy escort of a minimum of twenty mounted soldiers, a maximum of fifty.'

Drury pursed his lips. 'Either way, that's a lot of armed men for a small group like ours to attack.'

'You will have Don Renaldo's nine men — and me.'

He looked at her steadily; her dark, liquid eyes were unwavering.

'We'll have to see about you, *señorita*. But I won't have the full nine *pistoleros*. I'll have to spread 'em out a little.'

'Perhaps if you told me your plan . . . ?'

He smiled thinly. She coloured with a quick flash of annoyance.

'You do not trust me? A ward of Don Renaldo and his personal emissary?'

'Not just a matter of trust, Consuela . . . '

'You mean because I am a woman,' she said with unconcealed contempt. 'I can ride and shoot and rope with any of Don Renaldo's *vaqueros*! I can beat any *americano*!'

'Well, let's just leave that for now, eh?' Drury felt uncomfortable with this young woman — he had her age figured at not much more than twenty, could be a little less. But she sure had a confidence he wasn't used to seeing in the women he knew. 'I need men stationed in the desert to help us across. They have to prepare the run for me, so I can't bring them into the actual rescue.'

'How many of these *trustworthy* men do you need in the desert?'

'Haven't figured it out properly yet — been waiting to get details of the move but I'd say four to six, more if I can spare 'em.'

She frowned. 'I cannot even begin to see what kind of plan you have in mind — and it seems you are not going to tell me. So I will make a suggestion: use Don Renaldo's *pistoleros* for your rescue attempt, keep your own men for the desert crossing which seems to have you worried.'

Drury snapped his head around towards her. 'If you knew the Desert Altar, you'd be worried, too.'

'Not if I had crossed it.'

'Hell, lady, that was six, seven years ago and I had an Apache to help me. I'm relying on memory now.'

'*And* the good will of Don Renaldo Montez!' she snapped. 'You will do as I suggest?'

'Well, it would work OK, I guess, but I still need details before I can decide . . . '

'I can tell you only what Don Renaldo's agents have discovered; the details could change as I mentioned.'

'I'm prepared for that.'

She almost smiled as she said, 'But not for me.'

'No,' he said flatly. 'Not for you.'

'Then you should not look a gift horse in the mouth, *señor*. I believe that is an old saying of you Anglos?'

'Yeah. But are you saying Montez *wants* you involved in this?'

'Of course. After all, I am General Herrera's granddaughter.'

7

Plans

The place was getting crowded, over-crowded, but the *vaqueros* seemed content to make their own camp down behind the bunkhouse near the well. Consuela de la Vega declined Drury's offer of a bed in the house and said she would spread her blankets in the *vaqueros'* camp.

Santiago had been very quiet at supper occasionally glancing up at the girl and Drury. Once the group of Mexicans had repaired to their camp, Santiago braced Drury outside where he sat on the bench, smoking his after-supper cigarette with Woody Maguire. The tall Mexican was accompanied by Conrads and Quick. Cole Fisher watched from the corral rail where he sat smoking silently.

117

'This woman has too much to say,' Santiago said straight off. 'She may be Montez's ward, but this is not Mexico — and I must remind you once again, *Kincaid*, that this is my deal. I am the one to do any negotiating and to make the decisions.'

Drury glanced up through exhaling smoke.

'Montez sent the girl to me.'

'That I do not understand, either! *Why?* When you are the one who stole his horses, apparently have been doing it for years.'

Drury shrugged. 'He knew that, but I never set out to kill his men while I was stealing his broncs, not like some of the other border ranchers. They rode in with the intention of killing as many Mexes as possible and if they didn't get away with many or *any* broncs, they still figured it was a good night. 'Sides, I gave him McLaine, the man who killed his nephew.'

Santiago shook his head, still not convinced.

118

'*And* I gave my word to pay for the horses when I finished this job for you and you paid me the five thousand dollars we agreed on.'

Drury's gaze was hard as he said this last, for he had the hunch that he would never see a single dollar of the money Santiago had offered.

'Never mind all that. You seem to have forgotten that I know your true identity and can ruin you.'

Drury smiled. 'You could if you spread the word to the army. But you won't. Not yet a spell.'

Santiago drew himself up even taller. 'Oh? You think not? You wish to put me to the test?'

'Up to you. But you set the army at my heels and you have no one who can show Herrera the way across the Altar.'

Santiago's face hardened. 'If I have to, I will change my plans. This happens to be the best way. For now. But I am flexible, Drury, and you would do well to remember it. Now, I wish to know exactly what the girl said to you.'

119

'No harm in your knowing. I'd figured to tell you later anyway.' And the rancher brought Santiago up to date, gesturing for Cole Fisher to come and join them.

When Drury had finished, Fisher said sullenly, 'I just hope you can find your way across that desert, Lieutenant — and you'd better! 'Cause I'll be with you every step of the way. You get us lost and that's where they'll bury you.'

Drury flicked his cigarette butt away into the gathering darkness and smiled crookedly.

'And where'll they bury you, Cole? About ten feet away after you've wandered in circles for three or four days?'

Fisher scowled. 'Just remember, you'll still be able to find your way if you have a bullet through your gunhand!'

He whirled and limped away, one leg still sore and swollen from the beating he had taken at the rancher's hands.

'You should heed Cole,' Santiago told

him. 'He *will* be with you all the way — both during the rescue and the desert crossing . . . ' He gestured to Conrads and Quick. 'We will all be with you. Every step of the way. So plan well, Drury, plan *very* well!'

He turned away, followed by his men and when they had gone into the bunkhouse, Maguire said,

'Once you get him across to the Gulf, he's gonna pay you off with a bullet, Dave.'

Drury nodded slowly: that was his notion, too. But he was already working on a solution to the problem.

Maybe that pay-off bullet would ricochet back on to the man who fired it . . .

* * *

The *vaqueros* took on the chore of breaking in the remainder of the horses and not only did a damn good job, but their efforts freed Drury so that he could get on with plans for setting up the crossing of the Desert Altar.

Maguire's injuries were healing, although he still favoured bruised ribs on his left side and limped a little because of a swollen right hip. He had braced Cole Fisher only once, down by the corrals when he was saddling his mount.

'I owe you, Fisher,' Maguire told him quietly, and Cole had grinned.

'Any time you wanna settle the debt, little man.'

'You'll know when.'

Fisher laughed aloud. 'After you break an axehandle over the back of my head, you mean?'

'That'd be too quick for you, you son of a bitch. You'll see me comin'. An' you won't be able to stop me.'

Fisher's smile faded and he started forward, but Maguire climbed aboard his mount and swung its rump so that Cole was knocked flying, sprawling on hands and knees in the gravel. As he started to scramble angrily to his feet, Maguire backed up the horse and it knocked him down again. By the time he had sat up, reaching for his six-gun this time, Maguire was cantering across the yard.

When the gun did come free of leather, Drury came out of the corral and kicked it from his grip, wagging an admonishing finger at the angry hard-case.

'Better check with your boss before you go after Woody, Cole. He's the man fixing things so we can cross the desert.'

Cole scowled and spat as he stooped to pick up his gun. 'I can wait — for you, too!'

Drury smiled crookedly. 'Shouldn't't've warned me, Cole. Now I'll be ready — might just leave you somewhere out there in the Altar. Just walk away from you in one of the dust hazes that blow up out of nowhere, maybe during the night. We shared enough trails behind Indian lines along the Yellowstone so you know I can do it. You'll never find water out there without me — think about it. Help you to sleep easy?'

Drury chuckled as he walked away, leaving Cole Fisher white faced and tense as a statue.

⋆ ⋆ ⋆

Maguire had bought up half a dozen mules in Tucson and some wooden water casks and the pack frames to carry them. There were ten casks, each holding fifteen gallons so strong mules were needed for when they were filled.

'Charley Mengels says they come from Tombstone, used to carryin' loads of ore,' Maguire told Drury.

'Then they should be OK. The casks don't have to be filled till you cross the border near the Organ Pipes. I can show you on a map where there are two hidden Indian wells. That'll give the mules a break, but after that they'll earn their keep.'

'Whatever you say, Dave. We'll have to carry tools as well.'

'A packhorse can do it and take plenty of full canteens. You'll need 'em

124

for coming back.'

'How much water will the broncs use on the way down?'

'Give 'em what you have to but no more. They'll be all right once they're on their patches of grass. We'll drive some in from the southern end, the rest from the north-east.'

Maguire looked at the crude and barely adequate map Drury had first drawn.

'You're gonna be zigzaggin' all over!'

'That's the way the Apache brought me. Most men hit the desert and try to cross it in a straight line, figuring it'll be shorter . . . All it is, is a short cut to hell.'

Maguire frowned but nodded slowly. 'These blobs you say are landmarks . . . '

'I'll give you sketches of their silhouettes so you'll know what to look for, describe 'em as I recollect 'em. There's no guarantee they'll be the same after six years. When that Altar wind blows and lifts that sand it's like a grindstone. You've never seen such weird rock shapes anywhere as you'll see down there.'

'We-ell — I hope I can find my way.'

'Me, too — otherwise we're all dead . . . '

★   ★   ★

Santiago demanded a copy of the map Maguire was using but when he saw it consisted only of a few ragged, unconnected lines his face darkened. He set his gaze upon Drury.

'Don't get smart with me, Drury! Where's the real map?'

'That's it, all anyone gets . . . '

'You damn fool! What're you trying to pull?'

'I draw you a map filled in with all the landmarks and waterholes, you won't need me any longer.'

Their eyes met and Santiago's nostrils were rimmed in white before he slowly nodded.

'I want my men there, with Maguire.'

Drury shook his head. 'Woody and

Mel and a couple of Montez's *vagueros* plus the girl if she insists, are all we'll need. Maybe half a dozen all told. We'll use the rest of the Mexicans and your hardcases on the rescue attempt.'

Santiago didn't reply, ignored Drury's word so well that for a moment the rancher wondered if he had actually spoken aloud or had only thought about it.

'Details of the rescue — you said you would work them out.'

'Yeah. Consuela is going into Tucson where she's s'posed to meet one of Montez's men with the latest information about the move. Until we get more accurate times and an estimate on how many riders are going to be guarding the wagon or whatever they use, I can't do much.'

'Why is it, do you think, that Montez now has all this access to such information when he didn't even know Herrera was still alive for certain until you told him?' Santiago sounded suspicious, more so than Drury would have thought necessary.

He shrugged. 'Apparently he was told on pretty high authority that Herrera was dead or close to dying. Now he seems to have tapped into things from another angle. Seems to have better access to the Hermosillo prison than the Mexico City one where they were supposed to have taken the general after kidnapping him from the train.'

'Someone was lying!' Santiago snapped. 'Herrera was not taken to Mexico City. He was taken to a secret location on *el Presidente*'s orders! There were . . . '

He stopped speaking abruptly, suddenly wary at the look on Drury's face.

'How d'you know that?'

Santiago recovered quickly. 'I have perhaps better contacts than the great Don Renaldo Montez! *My* contacts tracked down the general's true location and also gave me the information about his move which prompted me to come to you.'

Drury kept looking at him steadily. Something wasn't quite right here. If Santiago had such a good line into

Montegas' camp how come he didn't have more information about the move to Caborca . . . ?

And another thing: Consuela had never heard of anyone named Jason Santiago who was a nephew of the General, Carlos Herrera. She swore there were no 'Santiagos' in the family . . .

'One other thing, Drury — I *insist* that my men accompany the general on the desert crossing with your men. I will, of course, make tham available for the actual rescue attack, but afterwards, instead of heading back north across the border, they will go with you across the desert. There will be no argument about this! You understand?'

Drury nodded slowly. 'Sure. You're the boss.'

And Santiago actually smiled: those were words he had been waiting to hear for many days.

'As long as you remember that, you will be duly rewarded.'

8

The Man in Charge

When Consuela returned from Tucson, escorted by two of Montez's *vaqueros*, she had the news Santiago and Drury had been waiting for: the transfer of Herrera was on within a week.

'They have decided to try to draw as little attention to the move as possible,' she added in the lamp-lit parlour of Drury's house while she ate a slice of cold pie set aside for her by Cookie. She managed to do it delicately, holding a folded kerchief beneath her pie hand so as to catch any crumbs.

'Exactly what does that mean, *señorita*?' asked Santiago. His voice was tight, edgy. He looked narrow-faced and intense.

'Simply that instead of the big cavalry force they had originally intended, twenty to fifty men, they are now using only ten soldiers in an attempt to make it look like just an ordinary prison transfer of rebellious prisoners.'

'*Prisoners*?' queried Drury. 'There'll be someone else besides Herrera?'

She nodded, still dusty and tired from her long ride.

'Oh, yes. There will be six prisoners in the special wagon, my grandfather amongst them. He will not be named on the transfer list, or, at least, only given a fictitious name. I do not know what it is, but it hardly matters.'

'No. We know what he looks like.'

'Even after such a long time in the hands of Montegas' torturers?' sneered Santiago. 'But, you are right, *señorita* — the name does not matter, only the man.'

'All right. Woody and his men ought to have finished their chore in the Altar within two days, though nothing is certain in that hellhole,' said Drury.

'They will be returning here?' asked Santiago, his mouth unsmiling; he had been annoyed considerably because Drury had refused to tell him exactly what Maguire's job was to be — or where the rendezvous was planned.

'No. They'll meet us at the rendezvous when we bring the general in. I haven't allowed for all of your men to cross the desert with us, Santiago. There aren't enough horses for that. Not to mention food or water.'

The tall Mexican's face tightened even more.

'Then leave some of your men or the *vaqueros* you'd planned on taking. I want Cole at least riding with you. I warned you, Drury, I would not have any argument about this.'

'So you did. Well, I guess you're in charge . . . '

'That's not guesswork,' interrupted Santiago, his eyes burning. 'It is a fact that you had all better remember!'

The girl stiffened, brushing crumbs from her chin and wiping her hands on the kerchief.

'*I* will be riding with the rescue party

and also accompanying my grandfather across the desert.'

Surprisingly, Santiago smiled. 'Of course you will, my dear. It is only right that kinfolk should stick together.'

She frowned. 'You mean, you are still calling yourself the nephew of the General?'

Santiago spread his hands, suddenly, seeming in a much brighter mood.

'Certainly. Just because your part of the family has never heard of ours it does not mean the General is *not* my uncle.'

'I — do not think this is so, but . . . as long as we both have the same objective. To save the General . . . '

'Oh, yes, *señorita*, that we must do . . . Cole? Con?'

Drury looked up sharply at the man's tone and froze when he saw that Conrad and Fisher had drawn their guns. Quick stepped into the room from the darkened kitchen holding a shotgun.

'The hell's this?' breathed Drury.

The girl was on her feet, looking alarmed. Santiago still smiled.

'We will work out the details of the rescue now,' Santiago said, lighting one of his cheroots and easing back in his chair. He smiled at Consuela. 'My dear, move across and stand beside Cole, if you will.'

She looked quickly at Drury who had stiffened.

'What're you up to, Santiago?'

'Just taking precautions, Drury — just taking precautions. I have had enough of your riding rough-shod over me and decisions I try to make. You have grown far too big for your boots and it is time for me to tighten my reins upon you.' He gestured to the girl who hadn't yet moved. 'Consuela will be my hobble on you, Drury. You will share *all* of your plans with me and do what I say from now on. The girl, of course, will stay close to myself and my men ... very close. You understand?'

Drury's face was rock hard, his eyes

deadly, and he saw the small compression of Santiago's lips.

But he nodded just the same.

Santiago had outmanoeuvred him.

Once again, the tall Mexican was the man in charge.

*　★　*

It was a day to remember and, as the Mexicans and Indians had said many times in the past, a good day to die. *But only if you had to . . .*

It was a marvellous day, cloudless blue skies, hot but not uncomfortably so, even a small breeze slithering snakelike through the canyons with a hushed moaning sound, cooling the sweat on a man's flesh.

The banner of dust that rose from the rutted trail was not large, though larger than Drury had expected, considering the information Conseuela had given him. Still he studied it through the field-glasses and found there were a dozen horsemen, six in front, six at the rear, surrounding the lumbering prison wagon. A rifle-armed guard dozed in the high seat beside the driver who seemed to be constantly lashing at the team of ten mules with a long bullwhip.

The wagon itself was a four-wheeled affair, high off the ground so as to clear the rocks and other obstructions, making for fewer breakdowns and hold-ups. The back of the vehicle was partly heavy timber up to a height of about two and a half feet and above this it was made up of woven iron straps, including the roof. The door was also of woven iron and although he couldn't see them, he knew from Consuela that there were four heavy horizontal bolts secured by hand-sized brass padlocks and one vertical bolt sunk into an iron plate on the floor of the wagon, padlocked top and bottom.

Even if a band of attackers managed to take the wagon, they would have one hell of a job releasing the prisoners. Especially as the keys for all the locks were not carried with the wagon. They were to be sent on ahead by a relay of six special messengers, to Caborca . . .

★   ★   ★

One of the things that Montez's agent had found out was the secret route travelled by these messengers — changed frequently — and Cole Fisher was already lying in wait along this trail. The rider was to meet relief messengers at certain points, pass the keys in a sealed leather satchel and the new man would start off immediately on a fresh horse, riding it hell for leather until he came to the next waiting relay rider and so on until the keys were safely in Caborca where they would be waiting when the prison wagon arrived.

That was the theory.

Now, Cole Fisher waited in the sunbaked rocks above the trail that the third rider would use. One of Montez's *vaqueros* was with him, a young Mexican, darkly handsome, nervous, but determined to play his part well.

He suddenly pointed to the cloud of dust drifting down the meandering trail through this cactus-studded region.

'Get ready,' growled Fisher, settling himself more comfortably in the wind-torn trough in the rock where he waited, snugging the curved brass plate of the rifle-butt firmly against his right shoulder.

He picked out a lower bend in the trail, flipped the specially mounted peep sight, and made his adjustments unhurriedly. This would not be the first rider he had ambushed — not even the tenth — and he had learned long ago that a man had greater success the cooler he remained.

He whistled softly behind his teeth, his lips parted, roughly following the tune of *Turkey in the Straw*, finger caressing the trigger as he waited for the rider to appear. The man came into sight suddenly, flogging his already lathered horse, skidding it around the bend, sending it hurtling down the last slope towards the flats. Half-way down,

Fisher's rifle crashed and as the echoes slapped across the dusty land, the rider suddenly reared up in the saddle, clawed wildly at the air and catapulted over the horse's swerving rump. The horse ran on but the man rolled twice and then stopped, not moving again. As the horse realized it was free of its rider, it tried to turn its head to see what had happened, slowing at the same time.

'Git on down, kid!' snapped Fisher, a new cartridge already in the breech, and the Mexican started to run down his side of the slope to where the panting horse was beginning to slow.

The kid held a sealed leather satchel in his left hand and used it for balance so he could get up some speed. He lunged at the horse, which was getting ready to run from him, caught the trailing reins and was in the saddle quickly. He untied the twin to the leather satchel he carried from the cantle, flung it to the ground and replaced it with his own: it contained a set of false keys and would be delivered by the other waiting relay riders to the prison authorities at Caborca. They would have no reason to suspect that these were not the genuine keys for the prison wagon and so no alarm would be raised . . .

The young Mexican raked the already bloody flanks of the horse with his spurs and it lunged away with a wild whinny, continuing on down the meandering trail. Fisher came sliding down the slope, picked up the satchel of keys and then moved to the body of the rider he had shot, dragged him into the rocks and covered his body with bushes he had cut earlier, then he collapsed a small cutbank over them.

Still whistling almost soundlessly through his teeth, he shouldered his rifle and walked back up the slope to where his own horse waited.

By the time he reached the rendezvous the others would have the wagon in their command — and he would hand over the keys and the prisoners could be set free.

Meantime, the Mexican kid would deliver his satchel of false keys to the rider waiting for the man who had been ambushed, and he in turn would take them to the next rider. For security reasons the riders were changed each time prisoners were moved by wagon so it was highly unlikely they would know each other . . .

* * *

Drury could only hope that Fisher and the young Mex with him had carried out their part successfully, because it would be hell's own job trying to break out the prisoners from the wagon without a set of keys for the padlocks.

The wagon and its escort had now moved into the first of the shadowed canyons and Drury checked his rifle and pistol loads one more time — army habits died hard, but what had been boring routine during training had saved many a man's life. Satisfied with his weapons, Drury slid down from the rock where he had been lying, faced his men. Con Conrads was there amongst Montez's Mexicans and Quick was with the second squad of raiders on the far side of the canyon, awaiting his signal to attack.

Santiago was well out of things — he had a habit of working well away from any danger — and he would no doubt have the girl with him.

'The wagon's entering the first canyon and ought to be at the crosstrails in ten minutes,' Drury told the men quietly. 'Check your weapons one more time — *Do* it, Conrads! Just do it! — and follow me, quickly, but carefully. We don't want any injured horses here.' He repeated the orders in Spanish to make sure that the Mexicans understood, then heeled his buckskin forward, out of the draw where they had waited, and into an arroyo that cut into the second canyon at an angle.

Passing a huge boulder balanced atop a pinnacle of grey-brown rock, Drury took a handful of sotol twigs protruding from his rifle scabbard and touched a match to them. They flared immediately and were just green enough to give off a thin trail of smoke. He tossed them up on to the balanced rock, his signal to the second group to start their move towards the crosstrails.

The horses' hoofs echoed some within the dry wash because of the high, narrow walls, but when it widened into the arroyo the noise was reduced. Considerably. Not that it was a problem here for they could hear the growing thunderous rumble of the heavy wagon as its iron-tyred wheels crushed rocks beneath them and the outriders' saddle chains and gear rattled and creaked.

They could smell the dust raised by the wagon, blowing towards them which was good, because any sounds they did make would not be carried back to the prison wagon. The crosstrails were in a wide part of the canyon, inches deep in loose sand that had collected there because of the meeting of the swirling winds, making a kind of whirlpool in the air.

Normally the sand was inches deep but, this time, Drury and his men had dug two long trenches a couple of days earlier, covered them with interlaced brush, and then concealed this under a thick layer of sand. This part of the country was rarely travelled by anyone, not even the *rurales'* patrols, and was mainly used only by the prison transfer wagons.

Drury, feeling the tension keeping his belly tied in a knot, looked up at a low bench across the way, saw enough movement to convince him that the second group was in place in the deep shadow, waiting . . .

The sounds of the wagon and the crack of the driver's bullwhip reached them. There were streams of rapid curses in Spanish, an occasional honking protest from a mule as the lash raised dust and a little blood on its grey hide.

Then suddenly the curses grew

louder and more violent and desperate. Drury warily raised himself up in the stirrups so that he could see over the rock where he waited. He smiled thinly.

Many voices were shouting now and horses whinnied and mules honked. The rumbling of the wagon wheels had stopped — because they were buried to the axles in the deep sand trenches Drury and his men had dug earlier.

It would take dynamite to move that heavy wagon out of its present predicament.

Drury settled back in the saddle, raised his hand and swept it forward. His group surged out of their cover and at the same time the second group came thundering down the far slope, trapping the stunned, bewildered Mexicans between them, the massive prison wagon tilted far to the left, mules straining futilely against the harness.

9

A Day For Dying

The Mexican soldiers were well trained. They immediately abandoned the desperate attempts to free the bogged prison wagon and turned to face their attackers.

Three men dismounted from the foremost group of six, knelt and aimed and fired a volley, followed an instant later by another volley from those still mounted. Two of Montez's *pistoleros* pitched from their saddles and a horse spilled a third man. The rear group of soldiers formed a strung-out line and fired their volley, too, bringing down three *vaqueros* and their horses.

Montez's men fired wildly but fast and furiously with their repeating rifles, aided by Quick and Drury and Conrads. The lead stormed through the ranks of the mounted Mexicans and two pitched wildly without a sound; a third fell, hanging half out of the saddle but clinging desperately to the horn as his horse bolted, carrying him away from the fighting. Another horse went down thrashing in front of two hard-riding soldiers and there was a chaotic pile-up.

Riders met hand-to-hand and the *rurales* had the advantage here for they carried sabres. They cut and slashed with cold precision and the screams of men hacked with the curved blades were chilling in the way they echoed from the canyon walls.

'Break clear!' bellowed Drury, having warned them before the attack not to get close enough for the soldiers to use their sabres. '*Break clear, you fools!*'

He parried a slashing blow with his rifle, sparks bursting briefly as the blade struck the barrel. Drury bared his teeth and, still holding his rifle in both hands, slammed the butt savagely between the Mexican's eyes. The man reeled back, his face split open and a mask of blood. He fell and was trampled by his own horse. Drury stretched out along his horse's back, fumbling to push fresh cartridges from his belt through the Winchester's loading gate.

Something burned across his back like a bullwhip's lash and he felt the tug at his shirt as the bullet passed. Too damn close! He weaved the buckskin, using his knees, looked up in time to see a blade sweeping at his head, the soldier obviously meaning to decapitate him.

There was only one place to go — and Drury went in a sprawling fall to the ground, rolling swiftly away from the thundering hoofs of both the buckskin and the Mexican's mount. The soldier almost fell with the effort behind the blade which hissed through empty air and for a moment he hung precariously from his saddle, looking into the cold eyes of Drury who was still skidding on his back. The rancher thrust the rifle up one-handed and triggered, blowing the man clear out of the saddle. Then he continued to roll away until he found a place clear and safe enough for him to spring to his feet again. He whistled the buckskin to him, leapt into the saddle, and spurred back into the fray which was now like a battle of medieval times he had once seen illustrated in a history book. Only an occasional weapon now discharged and mostly six-guns at that — best for close-in combat such as this — mostly it was cut-and-thrust on the part of the soldiers, while Montez's men parried the blows.

Then, as Drury used his own Colt, wounding a *rurale*, he heard a steady roll of gunfire coming from back up the trail: the fighting had moved on ahead of the bogged wagon. He hauled the buckskin clear of the mêlée and squinted through the pall of dust.

There were two men — the driver and his guard, he thought — standing on a rock near the tilted wagon, shooting through the gaps in the woven iron straps. *They were slaughtering the prisoners!*

Drury spurred the wild-eyed, sweating, lathered buckskin forward and it hesitated, not wanting to get back into the crush of the battle; its hide was already bleeding in a half-dozen places from minor wounds. But the animal responded to a second spurring and Drury stood in the stirrups, thumbing the hammer of the Colt, the blast of powdersmoke blowing back into his eyes, momentarily blinding him.

But when it was clear he saw the driver was down, writhing in the sand up against the slanted bars of the wagon. Even as he watched, two bony, filthy, broken-nailed hands reached through the gaps and fastened about the man's thick neck. The guard moved in an effort to shoot the homicidal prisoner and then saw how close Drury was, spun and fired under his arm. The rancher heard the the *thrummm* of the lead, triggered twice even as the guard poked the smoking muzzle of his own gun through a gap in the iron-strapping and fired. The guard spun away, falling out of sight behind the wagon.

Where the hell was Fisher with the keys! thought Drury as he reined down, hipping in the saddle to look at the fighting behind.

It was over. Four soldiers, at least two of them wounded and sagging in their saddles, were hightailing it out of the canyon, taking the other crosstrail, intent only on flight. Some of Montez's men fired after them and one man was knocked from his horse but the others rode on.

'Get after them!' bellowed Drury hoarsely, waving his arm. 'We can't have survivors!'

A bunch of the *pistolero-vaqueros* spurred after the men with wild yells, waving their weapons. Conrads, holding a bloody kerchief to one side of his neck, and Quick came riding up, awkwardly tying a kerchief about a wound in his upper arm.

'They tried to kill the prisoners,'

Drury said, dismounting and running on rubbery legs towards the wagon. As he passed the surviving seven mules of the team, he called to the others to cut the animals loose and then skidded to a stop beside the wagon.

The man who had reached through the bars to strangle the wounded driver had succeeded, but he had died himself in the process. There was a stiff grimace set on his sunburned face that might have been a final smile of triumph . . .

There were three dead prisoners, including the man who had killed the driver. All the others had been shot, two of them pleaded with Drury to open the wagon. The third man was older, showing lots of grey streaks in his lank, nit-infested hair, his gaunt face made even gaunter by a sparse beard, clogged with old food and other filth. The eyes were dark and glittering and they stared hard at Drury.

'*Judas priest!*' Drury hissed. 'General Herrera . . . ?' Surely this emaciated, corpse-like man couldn't be the strutting, hard-muscled *revolutionario* who had dug the three bullets out of him in that hideout in the sierras all those years ago . . . ?

But the man nodded tiredly, almost imperceptibly and Drury tightened his lips. 'Kin — caid,' he rasped.

'Here,' said a voice behind Drury. 'Set him loose.'

Drury turned to find a dust-spattered, sweating Cole Fisher standing there, holding out the satchel that contained the keys to the wagon's padlocks.

'You're late — missed the fight.'

Cole grinned tightly. 'Saw it from the rim. Figured you were doing all right without me risking my neck.'

Drury smiled crookedly, cutting the sealed satchel open with his clasp-knife blade.

'Recollect you did that when we tangled with Spotted Horse up on the Sweetwater Rim. And there was a place called Owl Creek near Wind River Canyon where I seem to remember you managed to find some chores away from the fighting, too.'

Fisher's mean eyes narrowed. 'I was a scout — din' see I had to risk my neck once I led you blue-legs to the Injuns.' He reached up and lifted his hat, tugging at his wheat-coloured hair. 'And I've still got my scalp!'

Drury said no more, fumbled out the keys and between them they got the heavy door of the cage open and helped the wounded prisoners out. One man would die before sundown, Drury figured, but the other would likely survive. General Carlos Herrera's wound was not serious — a deep gouge across his thin chest — but the man appeared to be so malnourished and weak and suffering the effects of past tortures that Drury wondered if he would live through the arduous and horrific journey that lay ahead of him.

'Hell,' the rancher breathed as he looked at the living skeleton, then glanced around at the dead and dying men strewn about the canyon.

'Don't tell me all this has been for nothing!'

* * *

Montez's men reported back that they had 'caught up with' the fleeing wounded soldiers. They said no more but Drury knew the men were dead. So much the better — it would be quite some time before the wagon was missed as there were no check-in places along the trail. They took the extra stores that had been stowed in the wagon under the floor, selected a couple of quiet horses that had once belonged to dead men and made travois for both Herrera and the surviving wounded prisoner, Chavez. The other man had lived little more than an hour after his rescue.

Cole Fisher was doing his best to take charge but Drury quietly gave his orders and they were obeyed by Montez's men who had been told to do as the rancher wished. They would now return to Montez with their own wounded and lists of dead.

'I am reluctant to report to Don Renaldo that his ward is not in a safe situation, *señor*,' said the leader of Montez's men, a middle-aged *vaquero* named Romero.

'I give you my word she will be safe.'

Romero studied Drury's powder-and-trail-stained face for a long time and then nodded gently. 'As you say, *señor*. It is your guarantee that she will be safe — against your life.'

Drury nodded. 'I understand that. Tell Don Renaldo not to worry. I will see she returns to him safe and well.'

Romero thrust out his hand and Drury shook briefly.

'It has been an honour fighting you all these years, Señor Drury — and this time to fight alongside you. *Adios*. Or, perhaps, *hasta la vista* — for I will surely see you again if any harm comes to Consuela.'

'Let's make it *adios* for now.'

Romero and his men rode out and Drury turned to the others, mounted and waiting, the wounded men in the slanted travois. He swung wearily aboard the buckskin.

'Let's go, *amigos*. It's a long hard trail.'

'Hope you know the way, Lieutenant,' said Cole Fisher with a crooked lift to one corner of his mouth.

'Just tag along, Cole — just tag along . . . '

★　★　★

They had to keep to rough country where few people lived. Mostly it was Indians who managed to scrape a living in this harsh land, Apaches in hiding from American bounty hunters and undercover lawmen, hunting them for scalp money or because of crimes they had committed north of the border.

There were few signs of them and no one saw any living thing, not even the few hardy animals that managed to survive here. Just the same, there was the feeling of being watched and

157

stalked and Drury warned the men to keep a sharp look out.

'Our horses are worth a fortune to those renegades. Half of them are afoot and they'll take any risks to get a mount of their own.'

Cole Fisher unsheathed his rifle. 'The man who gets my bronc will only have it over my dead body.'

'That's the way they'll take it if they decide they want it,' Drury told him and they rode on in silence, alert, guns flashing in the sun.

At camp that night Quick said he heard a sound near the hobbled horse and blasted the night apart with a double-barrelled charge from his shotgun. He swore he heard a cry of pain but there was no blood or body, though next morning Conrads found one of the tethering ropes sawn half-way through.

But there was no further attempt to steal their horses and they swung way south so as to miss Caborca by twenty miles. Fisher griped about it.

'Man, that puts us into the desert

more than a day early! It's gonna be hard enough crossing it without starting early.'

'They just might've heard about the prison wagon by now. It's not likely, but some rider coming through might've found it and gotten word to 'em. I'm not prepared to take the chance. Not with him along.'

Drury gestured to the wounded Herrera who was muttering unintelligibly. They had doctored the wound, using natural plant juices to cleanse it and it really wasn't very serious. Or wouldn't have been in a man who had his health or even *half* his health. But in someone like Herrera who had suffered torture and malnutrition and God alone knew what kind of other ill-treatment, it was almost as bad as if the bullet had penetrated a lung.

'He could sure do with a sawbones and a stay in an infirmary but none of that's possible so meantime we do the best we can for him. And that includes staying away from any town or two-men-and-a-dog village that could pass along the word to Montegas' men that we passed this way,' Drury said.

'You make sense, OK,' admitted Fisher grudgingly, 'but I ain't no desert man and I aim to spend as little time in this Altar as possible.'

'Hell, this isn't the real Altar,' Drury told him. 'This is a picnic spot, compared to the northern part we have to cross.'

Fisher swore. 'Goddamnit, I'd just as soon put a bullet through Herrera and be done with it!'

'Forget it, Cole — and I mean *for-get* it!'

Fisher's eyes pinched down and his mouth tightened. It was clear he had a built-in fear of deserts that Drury hadn't known about. Mind, there hadn't been many real deserts up north when he had known the man in the army. But it was knowledge worth stowing away.

Who knew when it might come in handy . . . ?

* ★ ★

There was a smaller town north-west of Caborca called San Francisco which they also had to skirt and this meant going south again and across a river called the Coyote. It was mostly sand and quicksand and there was a brief moment of drama when Quick's horse strayed off the track and began to sink. But the others' ropes brought animal and man safely to firmer ground and Drury was interested to see that Quick, too, was afraid of desert country. In fact, he had already had to warn the man several times about drinking his water too quickly.

It was slow progress and the long way round, but the safest trail Drury knew and in the early morning two days later they reached the rendezvous amongst some rocks that had been carved into weird shapes by the desert wind: some looked like the fins of giant fish, others resembled nothing that they could be compared to, while still others, silhouetted against the rising sun, took on writhing shapes whose shadows sent grasping tentacles writhing across the desiccated land.

Out of the glare rode Santiago and Consuela de la Vega.

She went straight to the travois containing Herrera, knelt and began washing the injured man's face, speaking quietly to him. Santiago smiled, obviously pleased and relieved to see them.

'So your plan worked, Drury. Congratulations.'

'A lot of men died, Santiago.'

'A lot of men *had* to die for it to work.'

Drury nodded. 'Yeah, well, Herrera's not in such good shape. We ought to rest up here for a spell to let him gain some strength before we push on.'

'Out of the question! The boat will not wait. If we are not there on time it will sail and we will all be trapped! If Herrera can make it this far, he can make it the rest of the way, surely.'

'Well, I wouldn't bet on it . . .' Drury began and then suddenly the girl gave a startled cry and jumped to her feet, staring down at the wounded man on the travois, his gaunt face cleaned of filth, the sparse beard plastered to his wrinkled flesh.

'What's wrong, Consuela?' the rancher said, hurrying forward. 'Has he taken a turn for the worse . . . ?'

She stared at him looking horrified, unable to speak for a moment.

'Well, answer, woman!' snapped Santiago impatiently.

Consuela's small hands knotted into fists down at her sides and she looked very pale as she spoke directly up into Drury's wolfish face.

'I do not know who you have brought me, Señor Drury, but it is not my grandfather!' She pointed at the ravaged, wounded man with a trembling hand. 'That is not General Carlos Herrera!'

10

First Grave

'This man recognized me when I dragged him out of the wagon,' Drury said. He called me 'Kincaid' — not Drury. I take that to mean he recognized me from the time I rode into his rebel camp with three bullets in me . . . He *has* to be Herrera, Consuela.'

The girl shook her head stubbornly.

'He is not my grandfather. He — resembles him, but it would be hard to tell from his features after all he has been through. And this man, whoever he is, appears to have been through much . . . adversity.'

'Then why do you say he is not the general?' asked Santiago stiffly. He seemed edgy, looked around to make sure his men were close by.

Consuela looked from Santiago to Drury.

'He used to sit me on his knee and I used to play with the bright gold buttons on his tunic. I learned how to undo them . . . beneath — here' — she indicated an area just below the hollow of her throat. 'He had two moles one on top of the other, rather large. They looked like a figure eight or, as I used to call them, a brown snowman. This man does not have any such mark.'

Santiago made an impatient gesture. 'Now how the hell could you tell what he has or hasn't had? Look at the scars and filth on him . . . '

'I have washed the filth away. The scars do not reach that part of his chest. There — is — no — mark! Therefore, he cannot be my grandfather.'

'By God, we'll soon see!'

Santiago strode angrily towards where the wounded men lay. Chavez was conscious and watching silently, sipping water from a tin mug occasionally. His sunken eyes followed Santiago as the

Mex knelt beside the man Drury had believed to be Herrera and reached for him, ripping away the rotten fabric of what remained of his prison jacket.

Drury reached down, grabbed Santiago by the collar and heaved him back angrily, sending the man sprawling on his back.

Then a gun barrel ground against his spine and he heard the sneer in Fisher's voice as the man said:

'Now you just calm down, Lieutenant. This ain't your party no longer.'

Santiago scrambled to his feet as the girl hurriedly knelt by the wounded man. The tall Mexican's eyes were blazing with hate and he hissed at Fisher,

'Kill him! *Now*!'

Even Cole Fisher looked surprised at the order. Con Conrads' features remained blank and Quick drew his own gun but Fisher frowned at Santiago. He gestured to the shimmering heat waves and the furnace-hot desert. 'Still a long way from the Gulf, Jace.'

166

Santiago swore, reached out and snatched the Colt from Cole's hand. 'I — said — *kill* — him!'

He lifted the gun, thumbing back the hammer and Drury slammed the inside of the man's forearm, knocking the weapon aside as it fired, the bullet kicking sand over the kneeling girl and her wounded charge. She gave a cry of alarm but by then Drury had the gun in his hand and slammed it across the side of Santiago's head. The man crumpled and then Fisher punched Drury in the kidneys and as his legs buckled, Con Conrads hit him with his gun barrel, his hat rolling off as he sprawled in the sand, semi-conscious.

Fisher picked up his gun and kicked Drury casually in the ribs.

'I told you to calm down, Lieutenant.'

Drury rolled and sat up groggily, holding his throbbing head. Santiago moaned but made no move to get on his feet. Cole Fisher stood with feet spread, the gun cocked in his hand.

'Now what we gonna do, Lieutenant? If you've grabbed the wrong man . . . '

'He said his name was Herrera and he knew me as Kincaid . . . '

The girl had dusted sand from the chest of the wounded man. She had bandaged it and rubbed in salves from the medicine-box she had brought with her.

'See for yourself. There is no mark. No sign where it could have been and perhaps removed during his — interrogation.'

Drury, still a little dazed, had to agree. He turned towards Chavez, knelt unsteadily.

'Is that Herrera?'

Chavez didn't even glance towards the old man. '*Sí* — I theenk so.'

'Hell, man, you *think*! You were in prison with him! You ought to *know*!'

Chavez shook his head slowly, coughed, grimacing as he clutched his chest with some inward pain. His breathing was hoarse and wheezy.

'They put him in the wagon at

Hermosillo and say he ees Herrera . . . We had all been take from different parts isolation, punishment yard . . . none of us — know each other.'

'There goes that theory,' Fisher said and by then Conrads and Quick had helped Santiago up and had given him water.

The tall Mexican steadied himself against Conrads and glared his hatred at Drury. Cole Fisher stepped in front of Santiago.

'Looks like the gal's right, Jace. No sign of that mark.'

'Then we will have to ask the man himself.' Santiago's speech was slurred and he started forward, but suddenly tightened his grip on Conrads and put his free hand up to his swollen bleeding head. 'If this man is a decoy, we do *not* need you, Drury, because there would be no point in going to the Gulf . . . So — we will settle things soon.'

'He is still unconscious,' Consuela said, standing firmly beside the wounded man as if she would protect him with her life. 'He cannot be wakened! Any rough treatment will kill him.'

'Then we will wait.'

'Can't,' said Drury and all attention turned to him. 'Whether that's Herrera or not, Montegas is gonna send an army after us. If it is the general, he'll want him back. If he's a decoy, he'll want him dead — and us, too. We can't stick around here. We have to keep moving now.'

Santiago's gaze was steady and full of hatred but slowly he nodded. 'You make good sense, Drury. All right. You have a reprieve . . . '

'Do you not recognize your — 'uncle', señor?' asked Consuela sardonically.

'Allowing for what he has been through, I would have said there was no doubt about his identity.'

'That is not quite the answer to the question . . . '

'It is all you are getting. Now be quiet! I am tired of all this questioning of my orders! *I am in charge*! You will all do as I say from now on or there will be more than two travois necessary!'

He glared around but strangely no one seemed intimidated and, muttering angrily, Jason Santiago pulled free of Conrads' grip and stumbled across to his horse where he took his canteen and drank deeply.

Drury was about to warn the man that it was a long, long way to the first of the Indian wells, but decided against it.

If Santiago was in charge, then he ought to know what he was doing . . . To hell with him. Drury had bigger worries to keep his tired brain busy.

* * *

The travois were a problem. They rode well enough over the sand but there were areas where chunks of old lava and pumice-rock poked through or lurked just beneath the surface. These, if they hit the trailing poles, jarred the wounded men and once almost upset Chavez's travois.

Maybe he could ride a horse in another day's time, but there was no question of Herrera doing that. The trails left behind were hard to cover up although Cole Fisher did a pretty good job. But he knew Montegas would call in desert Indians to help with the tracking and he was not confident he had hidden the grooves cut by the travois poles well enough to fool them.

'We'll have to push it a mite harder,' Drury said. 'We've still got a little time. If no one stumbles across that prison wagon, it won't be missed till sun-up tomorrow, so we've had a good run, but we can't afford to lose any ground.'

Santiago put his mount in alongside Drury's buckskin.

'Then here is where you start to earn your money!'

Drury gave him a crooked grin. 'What money?'

He didn't have to explain and Santiago merely laughed coldly and dropped back alongside the girl. He had placed Conrads and Quick either

172

side of Drury, not trusting the man, while Cole Fisher dropped back to try to cover their tracks as well as he could.

Drury had refused to hand over his weapons after the small fracas earlier, although Santiago had demanded he do so angrily and with many threats — which were meaningless, because he simply *had* to keep Drury alive until they had crossed the Altar.

'There are still Indians about and they'll be after our horses and grub. We all need to be armed, because when they hit, they'll come fast and there won't be any time for handing out weapons to those who don't already carry them. I keep my guns or the whole kit-and-caboodle ends right here.'

Santiago curled a lip.

'By God, I will have a reckoning with you, Drury! And it will be a *dead* reckoning!'

That came as no surprise to Drury — but he had his own ideas about their reckoning, when and where and how it would happen . . .

173

★   ★   ★

If a man knows a trail that leads to water in the desert, or even if he *thinks* with good reason that it leads to water — he's a blamed fool if he leaves that trail.

Most deserts have hidden water-holes somewhere, perhaps not always with water in them, but these are generally known to local animals — and to local human inhabitants or travellers through the area. Birds and animals will come to drink at such places, may even lead men to the water. And local-living Indians will also come to drink.

So Drury took a chance he knew he shouldn't by rights take. He deviated from the trail as he remembered it, shown to him by old Crooked Tree. He did this for a purpose — he was testing Santiago and his men, for he had a hunch that the tall Mexican knew a little more about the desert than he was letting on. There had been hints, quick words spoken in argument when Drury had deliberately set a verbal trap to achieve just such a reaction.

He had a notion that Santiago had passed this way before. Or had at least been briefed on it.

Which posed the question: if the man knew his way around the Altar, or even part of it, why did he need to make a deal with Drury? Perhaps the Mexican knew only the southern part of the desert and needed Drury to get him across the north-west section that the Spaniards long ago had named *el Purgatorio* — Purgatory, certainly a corner of Hell itself. Yes, that was possible, but Drury realized that to survive, he had to know everything possible about Santiago. The man was sly and cunning, rather than smart, and there was a coldness to him, a willingness to kill, that was drawing closer to the surface with each new confrontation.

A man passing through wild country *must* be aware of everything about him, all the warning signs of nature, be it darkening skies or dust-devils whirling on the trail ahead, or the sudden flight of birds from a thicket or the whims of human beings.

Restless, open eyes, keen ears, every sense alert . . . these were the things that helped a man survive.

Santiago said nothing when Drury slanted away from the logical trail but Drury watched, amused, as, one by one, Conrads, Fisher and Quick all approached the Mexican and spoke with him earnestly. Santiago showed no emotion, said something briefly to each man, and they dropped back to their positions.

The girl rode between the horses pulling the travois, totally in Drury's hands. Chavez seemed to be recovering well, but Herrera — for want of another name — was making no visible signs of progress.

Drury set his weary buckskin alongside Consuela, seeing the sweat on her, the drawn mouth and flaking lips.

'Trust me, Consuela,' he said quietly.

'No matter how crazy or dangerous things that I do appear, trust me and I'll get us through this.'

Her eyes were reddened from the dust but their stare was steady and after a moment she nodded.

'I trust you, Drury.' Her voice was hoarse.

'Good. How's the old man doing?'

She frowned. 'He seems worse but . . . ' She paused and shrugged.

'But?' he said, sure she wanted to say something else but she shook her head and he rode away to the lead again, swinging slowly back towards the trail he wanted.

Fisher came up, face white-rimmed with alkali, eyes hard.

'I never heard of water bein' in this direction out here.'

'Not your country, Cole. But I did kind of slip direction there. My mistake.'

'Yeah, it was. I wouldn't make too many more, Lieutenant. Jace has about reached the end of his patience.'

'Now you've spoiled my chance of

getting a good night's sleep.'

'Joke all you want, but you could be laughing your way right into hell!'

The man dropped back and started covering the travois trails again. Drury smiled to himself.

The first sign of edginess and uncertainty, he thought. *Bueno!*

★   ★   ★

Drury's calculated and deliberate meandering from the trail had given him something of a scare. A landmark he remembered wasn't in the place it should be and instantly he felt a lurch in his belly, cursing himself for a fool. He ought to know by now that haphazard desert travel led only to one place — an unmarked grave. But he had taken a chance simply to prove a point — and he *hadn't* proved it very satisfactorily — and now he was in trouble.

But, hell almighty, how could a mountain ridge with a pinnacle half-way along disappear?

It became obvious even to Consuela, after a while, that Drury was making some chancy moves, riding off ahead to the nearest rise, standing in stirrups, obviously looking for something he couldn't find.

Santiago unsheathed his rifle and while Drury was standing on a broken rock, shielding his eyes from the glare with both hands, the Mexican fired a bullet close enough to lift dust from the rancher's hatbrim. Drury stumbled and had to leap down, falling to hands and knees in the sand. Santiago's next shot fountained sand between Drury's spread hands.

'If we are lost, you will not have to worry about dying of thirst, Drury!' he said.

'For Chrissakes! I'm taking bearings on landmarks I remember. And quit wasting ammunition. We might need it. And the gunfire might attract Injuns.'

'Stop wasting time then! Get us to water! Our canteens are almost empty.'

Drury dusted himself off, mounted

the buckskin again. Luckily he had seen something in the distance, in a more northerly direction than he remembered. He saw a mountain ridge, barren and grey as weathered clapboards, and it was the same lizard-shape he was searching for. Except there was no pinnacle where there should be.

But he recalled the old Apache telling him once that there was a lot of ironstone in this desert and tall outcrops — like pinnacles — were often blasted by bolts of lightning when electrical storms twisted and writhed through this dusty air. He had spoken of two ironstone chimneys he had seen explode before his eyes when struck.

Now Drury had to assume that this was what had happened to the pinnacle that had been on that ridge six years ago — always supposing the ridge he was now looking at was the right one . . .

But he had little choice and he led his party in that direction.

Luckily it turned out to be right and

from the top of the ridge he made his way down towards the next water-hole.

It was almost sundown when they came into the parched basin, dipped deeply in the middle. He halted the weary horse and dismounted stiffly. The others plodded up and Santiago looked around.

'Where the hell's the water?' he rasped and Drury pointed, starting forward.

'Judas, he must he loco with thirst!' growled Quick. 'There ain't nothin' out there . . .'

'Yeah, there is,' said Conrads. 'I can see it, barely throwin' a shadow but you can make out the cross.'

'Cross!' echoed Cole Fisher, squinting.

'Yeah — there's a grave out there. All by its lonesome.'

11

Grave by Grave

There was no body in the grave.

While Drury tossed aside the piled rocks, Cole Fisher walked around slowly looking at the bunch of owl feathers tied to the top of the crude weathered cross — and the three clay owls set in the sand around the grave.

'Aimed to keep the Injuns away, huh?'

Drury looked up, wiped sweat from his face and nodded.

'The owl is a sign of evil and fear to them. Figured it might work . . . lend a hand here, will you?'

Fisher snorted and walked away but Conrads and Quick started throwing off rocks and underneath were two shovels. Drury handed one to Quick and together they dug away the sand, the gunfighter looking more and more wary the deeper they went.

'What we gonna find here?' he asked.

'Couple of feet more and you'll see.'

Even as he spoke, Drury's shovel blade struck wood with a hollow thud. Quick snapped his head up, climbed swiftly out of the hole. Drury smiled, began scraping the sand away, knelt and lifted out several short boards about eighteen inches long, four wide and one thick. He reached down into the dark hole and tossed something out. Conrads jumped back, glimpsing only a head-sized shape coming towards it. It was a gunnysack — half full of oats for the horses.

'Clear away the rest of the sand,' Drury said, tossing out a sack of something that *clunked* dully and a can of beans rolled out.

Even Fisher helped, clearing away the sand, throwing out the short wooden pieces, then bringing up sacks of food and at either end, at the head and foot of the grave, were two wooden casks, sealed with nails and tar. They were heavy and the precious water they held sloshed almost musically.

There was a claw-hammer also buried in the grave and Drury used this to rip open the top. He removed it. As Quick rushed in to scoop up water, he pushed the man back.

'This one's for the horses. We'll fill our canteens from the other cask.'

They ate well, brewed coffee and topped up their canteens.

'Where're the fresh mounts?' asked Santiago, lighting one of his cigarillos which he had been rationing during the ride north.

'We'll get them in the morning. Now we have to work out guard roster.'

'Thought you said them owl statues'd scare away any Injuns?' growled Conrads.

'If they see them. If there're any watching they could come down for a looksee and decide to take our horses and maybe our scalps, and to hell with the owls.'

There were a lot of complaints but

the men finally agreed and Drury walked across to where Consuela had been tending to Chavez and the old man.

'I theenk maybe I try ride tomorrow,' said Chavez.

'We'll see.' Drury hunkered down beside the girl and indicated the oldster: 'How is he?'

She hesitated before answering. 'No better. I would have expected some slight improvement but he does not appear to be any closer to consciousness. He may already be in a coma.'

'From a slight wound like that? OK, I know he's not in the best of shape but — well, I guess you'd know better than me. And you're still not certain he is your grandfather?'

'I am certain he is not. I have not seen him for many years, of course, but there is that mark of the brown snowman . . . '

Drury turned to Chavez. 'Nothing you can add?'

'I am sorry, señor. I do not see heem

185

before the prison wagon.' He paused, frowned, opened his split lips as if to speak, but didn't say anything.

'What is it, Chavez? Anything at all that might help . . . '

The girl leaned closer and Chavez lowered his gaze, fumbled around some and then said, 'I — we hear long time — the General — he die.'

Consuela sucked in a sharp breath. Drury stiffened.

'How long back' he asked tightly.

'Time passes slowly in prison, señor. But I theenk — maybe six or seven weeks . . . '

'Not long after Herrera was kidnapped from his train,' Drury murmured. 'If that's right . . . then who the hell have we here?'

Consuela was already looking at the old man who resembled her grandfather. There were tears in her eyes as she turned towards Drury. 'I must know what has happened!'

'Yeah, I savvy how you feel, Consuela. But looks to me like we're going to have to wait for this feller to come out of his coma . . . '

Her white teeth nipped her bottom lip and she frowned thoughtfully down at the wounded man . . .

★   ★   ★

The horses were an hour's ride from the grave, the small grassy canyon where they were kept suddenly opening up almost beneath the feet of their mounts.

Santiago was not pleased when Mel Roberts stepped out from behind a rock, cocked rifle in hand. 'Howdy, Dave. Everythin' goin' okay?'

'So far, Mel. Have any trouble?'

'Nope. All quiet and the broncs have been browsin' and are ready to go.'

The fresh horses were all clustered together in a corner of the small canyon, watching the newcomers and their trail-weary mounts. Drury had to explain to Santiago that Mel had been left here to watch the relief horses in case Indians made a try for them.

'You got men at every pick-up place?' the tall Mexican asked.

Drury nodded. 'There's someone there.'

He looked around at his men and Cole Fisher pursed his lips. 'Best change saddles, I guess,' the hard-case said.

This they did, rehitching the travois to a new horse, Chavez insisting that he was now fit enough to ride.

A couple of spare saddles had been cached here and Mel rigged one on a quiet mount and helped the wounded man into leather.

'I can fight, too, I theenk.'

'If it comes to a fight, you'll get a gun,' Drury told him. Then, leaving their tired horses in the canyon they rode up on to the desert and continued their journey. The fresh mounts did not like the hot gritty winds of the desert after the cool of the sunken canyon and took a bit of settling down, but the group still made good time.

Until the old man suddenly sat up half-erect in the travois, crying out in a cracked voice that a sidewinder snake had slithered across his skinny legs.

No one at first thought anything about his crying out in a croaking though intelligible voice: they hurried to the travois and began tearing apart the blankets. Quick leapt away as something long and supple slithered free and across his boots. It wasn't a sidewinder, only a shingleback lizard but the man got such a fright that he drew his pistol and shot its head off.

'Judas *priest!*' he said, clutching at his chest. But the gunshot had frightened some of the new horses and they scattered. Santiago still being the only one mounted, he took off after them, Quick and Fisher running and shouting, trying to catch up with them, too.

The old man had been upended and lay on the sand; the girl was struggling to put him on his back while Conrads and Mel started gathering the blanket poles of the travois.

It was about then that Drury, stooping to pick up a crumpled blanket, paused, snapped his head around and looked at the old man. His head was cradled in the girl's lap and he was breathing hard and fast after his fright, his eyes wide open, no longer looking dull and droopy as they had been ever since his rescue. He was out of his 'coma'!

The girl met Drury's gaze as he knelt beside the wounded man.

'Time you did some talking, old-timer. And don't try to tell me you're General Herrera or I'll find a real sidewinder and put it into bed with you.'

'Drury!' Consuela said sharply. 'Whoever he is, he is still wounded and has suffered much.'

'That right, old man?' Drury asked in a hard voice. 'You suffered at Montegas' hands? Come on! It's about time you quit playing possum and told us just who the hell you are!'

'Drury, you must stop this bullying! He is — '

'He's a goddamn impostor and a lot of men have died because we believed he was General Carlos Herrera.' Drury leaned over the now frightened man and barked into his gaunt face. 'Just who the hell are you, feller? Now answer — and answer fast!'

The old man's rheumy eyes opened wide, seeking the girl, sensing she was on his side. '*Señorita*! I am truly the General . . .'

He stopped when she stiffened suddenly, face straightening.

'You are not my grandfather! Please do not lie to me any more!'

As he fell silent, Mel said, 'Dave — I dunno about you, but now could be a good time to move out . . .' He gestured to the distant men still chasing those horses that had run away, Santiago had dismounted now, too, and was waving his hat, trying to bring the horses to heel. 'If this really ain't Herrera, Santiago ain't got no use for you — *or any of us* — from now on.'

Drury watched as Santiago's men

tried vainly to corner the horses. His own mount was one of the bunch that had run off but there were still three here, and Chavez, who had not dismounted.

'The old man'll have to ride double with someone . . . '

'I'll take him,' Mel said.

'Is it necessary to run?' asked the girl.

'Yeah! Mel's right — Santiago won't need us if this feller is a stand-in . . . Let's go!'

Cole Fisher spotted them as Drury struggled to lift the old man up to the mounted Mel. He shouted and went for his gun and fired two fast shots. Santiago had let go his mount's reins and the horse whinnied and ran to join the others as Quick and Conrads started shooting, too.

Bullets whined overhead and the girl was pale as she crouched over her mount and spurred away, looking to see if Mel was following with the wounded old man. He was. Drury ran for the remaining horse, a skittish black with a smoke-coloured blaze between the ears.

Drury caught the reins, leapt into saddle and spurred after the others, Chavez calling to him to let him have a weapon. Mel threw the Mexican his rifle as he had enough to do trying to hold the old man in the saddle with him. Chavez caught it and started firing.

Fisher was running towards them shouting curses, followed by Conrads. Santiago was fuming and shooting wildly. His words drifted clearly to Drury — and hit him with such shock that he stopped levering his rifle and almost hauled rein.

'Kill the old man! Kill him — then the others!'

Why the old man first? Drury wondered then finished levering the shell into the rifle's breech as he threw the weapon to his shoulder and fired. Santiago's hat spun off his head and the tall Mexican dived for the ground.

Quick was kneeling, holding his six-gun in both hands, arms moving as he had Chavez on the run. He fired and the Mexican reeled in the saddle, managed to grab the horn, but hung at a precarious angle as his horse raced on after the others.

Sand spurted about the racing hoofs. Lead hummed above their heads. The horses were wild-eyed but stretching out now. Drury called for a change of direction and in a few minutes they were beyond the reach of Santiago's guns.

But the Mexican and his men were running for the horses now, desperate to catch them. Drury smiled.

'Lots of luck, fellers!'

Then he rode after the others, the wind burning his face as he came up alongside Chavez and straightened the man in the saddle. He saw the Mexican was badly hit under the ribs and would not last long. Chavez handed him the rifle with a weak smile.

'You — may — need thees.' Then he slumped and Drury couldn't hold him as he fell and tumbled across the sand.

He didn't move after he stopped rolling.

Juggling the rifle and ramming it under his stirrup strap, Drury snatched the flying reins of the riderless horse and brought it alongside. They might need it before they reached the next grave — or the next — or the one after . . .

There were five graves west of here and they had visited only one so far. He wondered how many of the others they would reach before Santiago and his men caught up with them? The plan had seemed simple enough: bury food and water, plant fresh mounts, and cross the Altar grave by grave . . .

But it was clear now that none of them was meant to reach the Gulf alive — and the answer lay with the mysterious old man.

12

No Talk — Just Bullets

Pursuit didn't come right away — and that puzzled Drury.

He had paused, climbed to the top of a surreal lava pile and raked the backtrail with his field-glasses. There was a pall of dust back there, but much further away than he would have expected. And much larger, also.

He climbed down and told the others. The girl was tending to the old man still and she glanced up as Mel said,

'Seems to me this is some kinda double-cross, Dave. Could Santiago have had men waitin' somewhere close by?'

Drury shook his head. 'Not out there. Nowhere to hide except in that sunken canyon. And you were there with the horses.'

'Perhaps,' spoke up Consuela as Mel made no answer, 'perhaps this Santiago waited for the soldiers.'

They stared blankly at her, and then Drury frowned as he slowly realized what she was implying.

'Seems to me, we better find out just who this old feller is — and what the hell he's doing, pretending to be Herrera.'

The old man opened his eyes, closed them briefly as Consuela washed away dust with a moist cloth, and then opened them again, looking up at Drury.

'I am called Rico Navarro. I am a thief and I was condemned to death for stealing political documents from the pig who calls himself Montegas.' He tried to spit but his mouth was too dry. The girl gave him a sip from a canteen.

'Mel — keep a lookout,' Drury said, tossing the man a rifle. He sensed the old man was about to tell them something important and although it was risky staying put, he didn't want to lose this moment. 'How come you're still alive, Señor Navarro?'

The old man almost smiled, but it was really little more than a twitch of the thin, dry lips.

'It seems I resemble General Herrera.'

The girl and Drury exchanged a glance and the rancher said, 'Chavez told us the general was dead.'

The old head nodded. Drury found himself listening for a creaking sound.

'This is true.' The rheumy eyes sought Consuela. 'I am sorry, *señorita*. But your grandfather died weeks ago ... he was — put to the torture after he was taken from his getaway train but ... ' The bony shoulders shrugged slightly. 'They say it was his heart ... '

Consuela brushed a hand across her eyes, nodded, and swallowed audibly before saying, '*Sí*, he did have a bad heart. That was one reason Don Renaldo tried to find out where he had been taken after his kidnapping

— but there was never any information . . . nothing at all.'

'No. He was taken to a secret political prison — I am ashamed to say that I am just a common thief, *señorita*, but I made a mistake and took those important papers, thinking I could sell them for a great deal of money . . . but no one believed me. They were sure I was a *politico* and had been sent by the rebels to steal the papers . . . I was given much torture, too, in the same room as the general. I saw him die . . . '

The cracked voice faded and there was silence except for the sounds of the desert: heat-cracking rocks, sand whispering as vagaries of breeze swirled grains together, the distant cry of a high-flying buzzard, the squeal of a rodent caught by talons or fang.

'There was great confusion and disorder. I was forgotten, left to hang in my chains . . . Montegas himself came and he shot the man who had been torturing the general at the time of his death . . . later, he turned to me and seemed to really look at me for the first time . . .

' 'What do we have here?' he said. 'I see General Carlos Herrera hanging in those chains.' Of course, no one knew what he meant at first, including myself. And then he laughed and began striding around the cellar, slapping his leg with that leather-covered steel rod he always carries. He turned on the others, who were all looking frightened — and that included me, also! 'Here is a man who resembles Herrera! Are you all blind! *Look! Look*, you fools! See?' Naturally they all said, '*Sí el Presidente*! We see!' Then he told them to give me some medical treatment and a wash — 'Not too much! We do not want it to be too apparent that he is not the pig Herrera!' And they took me and washed me and treated some of my wounds and gave me some food . . . and then I was taken to Montegas' office.'

Navarro paused, trembling at the memory. Consuela gave him more water, bathed his face once again.

'Okay, Mel?' called Drury and Mel Roberts told him that the dust cloud hadn't gotten much closer. 'We won't stay much longer,' Drury turned back to Navarro. 'Just tell us quickly how they had you stand in for Herrera — and why.'

'The 'why' is simple enough,' Consuela said quietly. 'Montegas did not want it known that my grandfather had died at his hands.'

Drury nodded and the old man confirmed the girl's observation.

'I was told my life would be spared if I did what they wished. They also promised to look after my family but I knew they lied. Long ago I had had word that my family had been killed in one of their raids. But I pretended I thought they were still alive and agreed to play the general. I saw here a chance to escape . . . '

'You called me 'Kincaid' when we got you out of the wagon.'

'You were described to me. They said

there will be a rescue attempt, led by a man named Kincaid. You must greet him by name . . . '

Drury frowned, not liking the implication at all. 'But that soldier tried to kill all of you prisoners . . . '

'He was supposed to wound me only lightly so I could pretend it was much worse and so make out that I was in great pain and fake a coma. I don't know why, but they did not want me to be questioned until we were deep into the Altar.'

Drury stiffened. 'They *knew* the escape route was that way?' The old man nodded and the rancher swore softly. 'I've been set up from the start!'

'By Santiago?' the girl asked.

'Yeah. Now what the hell goes on?'

He looked down as one of Navarro's broken, misshapen hands clawed at his arm.

'Señor, I think they mean for me to die in the desert. And it will look then as if I was killed in — in a rescue attempt staged by an American.'

'But I thought Montegas was trying to stay in the US's good books?'

'Up to a point — but if word got out that the general died under torture, the rebels would rise and nothing would stop them killing Montegas and all his men . . . This way, the *americanos* take the blame and the rebels would side with Montegas against the *Estados Unidos*.'

'He's not loco enough to go to war with the US!'

'Who knows what the madman Montegas will do?'

'But what the hell could he gain?'

It was Consuela who answered. 'There is a strong anti-American feeling in Mexico, Drury. It may not appear on the surface but deep down the people have never forgiven Sam Houston for wresting Texas from Mexico.'

'Hell, that was forty years ago!' But Drury paused before saying more: there were plenty of Americans who had never forgiven Mexico for The Alamo slaughter — and never would.

'I still can't see anything for Montegas to gain.'

'There are foreigners urging him on, señor,' said Navarro, breathing raggedly now. 'From a place called Europe . . . You will remember the pretender Maximilian who had the support of the French . . . '

'Well, I'm damned! This is a bit beyond me — I can't see just what I'm tangled up in here, but I figure that Santiago don't mean for any of us to get out of this alive.'

Drury stood and signalled Mel to climb down.

'We've got to move. If they catch us, there won't be any talk. Just bullets.'

Mel frowned. 'What's up, Dave? What've we done wrong?'

'Whatever Santiago wanted us to do — it was all wrong. Herrera's dead and this man's been used as a decoy but now they have to kill him — so we get the blame. And that means killing us so we can't talk, too . . . '

Mel started to swear, but remembered

the girl. 'I don't get it . . . '

'No time to figure it out now. Señor Navarro, it's gonna be hard on you. Whether that's really only a minor wound or not, you've had a mighty rough time and . . . '

'I will keep up, *señor* . . . I know they wish to kill me now so I have nothing to lose.'

So they roped Navarro to Chavez's horse and the girl rode close in on one side, Mel on the other. Drury covered their tracks as best he could, all the time remembering that Cole Fisher had been the best scout and tracker in the north when he had been in the army . . .

Now the man was tracking for Santiago.

★   ★   ★

The desert turned its fury upon them — yet, ultimately, it may have also helped their efforts to escape.

The wind grew hotter and suddenly

there was an overload of grit stinging their faces, causing their mounts to toss their heads and snort in annoyance. This increased and far ahead they could see wind-waves laden with grit sweeping towards them, curling over like the edge of some hazily seen sea-shore.

But the sting was such that it took their breath away, made them reel in the saddles, caused the horses to fight reins and spurs, turning so as to take the buckshot-raking wind on their bodies. The riders tugged up kerchiefs over their lower faces and Navarro's gaunt features were covered with a cloth from the line of his scant hair to below his bony jaw. The girl wrapped a blanket about his emaciated body. It was as well that he was roped to the horse, for he was so frail that the wind could easily have blown him completely off the animal's back.

It wasn't the usual kind of desert sand-storm. Most such dust-storms blotted out the sky, piled up drifts of sand and dust against anything that didn't keep moving. It worked its way inside clothing and even tightly closed mouths, sure as hell into the corners of eyes and nostrils. Most men figured there wasn't much worse than a sand-storm in the desert, unless it was thirst and starvation.

But a hot wind out of the south, carrying tons of grit and alkali in the badlands at the edge of the Altar was worse. The grit not only found the minute places where dust worked its way in, it *cut* and abraded and rubbed flesh raw. Then sweat and more grit stung the raked places and blood stuck flesh to clothing so that even when the storm had ended there were more hours of pain to face as precious water was used to help loosen these adhesions.

Horses suffered, too, perhaps worse than humans as raw patches appeared in every wrinkle and joint. They turned rump-to but stamped and tail-switched and whinnied in pain as pumice worked under the saddle cloth and rubbed back and spine raw.

Alkali burned their eyes and throats, filled hat-crowns and even their laps until they managed to get in behind a lava ridge and dismount. The horses reared.

'Hold the reins!' shouted Drury against the rising howl of the wind. 'Don't let 'em pull free or we're a goner!'

He helped the girl while Mel got Navarro untied and into a crevice of the lava. The grit hit the lava wall with a loud hissing noise that rasped away at the porous rock like a thousand files. They could still see the sun beyond the swirling brownish-white cloud above them, but it was no more than a flat white disc that looked something like a featureless moon. There was no heat in it but being trapped in the envelope of hot air from the wind gave them the sensation of stifling in a kiln.

Sweat oozed from their pores but was not there long enough for the grit to adhere to in a muddy paste, because it evaporated so fast. They were parched, every fibre in their bodies dehydrating rapidly. Soon they began to feel light-headed and their ears were clogged so they could barely hear each other shouting their alarms. The horses were giving more and more trouble, disoriented and affected just as badly as the humans. Soon it was impossible to hold them and they had to release their grips on the reins so as to avoid stomping hoofs.

The animals moved away only a few yards before they vanished from sight.

Drury pulled Mel back as he made to start after them, half rising and being hammered flat by the howling wind . . .

Time was meaningless and passed sluggishly.

Their minds became dulled to the deafening assault on their senses and they huddled closer to the lava rock, curling up, with the blend of grit and alkali and flaked pumice gradually piling up around their bodies . . .

★ ★ ★

It had started suddenly and it stopped even more suddenly. The noise was gone in an instant. Their hatbrims bent under the load of detritus the wind had dropped on them and they began to sneeze, dabbing at raw, dripping nostrils gently with any small area of neckerchief that had not been impregnated with grit.

They couldn't speak, rinsed out their mouths and throats with tepid, foul-tasting water. It took a lot longer to wash their eyes out so they could see properly.

There was no sign of their mounts but, incredibly, there was a line of riders closing in on the lava ridge from the north, and already they could clearly hear the muted thunder of the approaching horses.

13

Grave Five

Battered and exhausted, Mel and Drury grabbed their guns and brushed and blew to remove accumulated grit and dust. The girl put out her hand for a six-gun and Drury's eyes met hers briefly before he handed over his Colt.

Then Mel said, 'Relax, Dave — it's Woody with the spare mounts.'

Their relief left them kind of empty as their own sore eyes confirmed what Mel had seen. Woody Maguire came riding in on them with the spare horses from the second hidden canyon. He reined up in front of Drury, his face still showing the fading bruises and healing cuts left from Cole Fisher's beating. He coughed hard into a bandanna, grimacing.

'Figured you must've gotten caught

up in that wind-storm . . . mostly blew over the canyon but soon as it faded I got the hosses up. You look like you need 'em.'

'Good to see you, Woody,' Drury told him hoarsely. 'Didn't realize we were this close to the second grave.'

'Yonder,' Maguire said, pointing to a newly risen hump of sand and detritus. 'Take a little diggin' — so we'd best not waste time. I seen a smudge of dust to the south that looked more like a bunch of riders than the wind.'

He turned, hawked and spat into the sand, covering it quickly with a sweep of his boot.

'Santiago must've made up time,' allowed Mel, standing in stirrups and squinting, shading his eyes. But he couldn't yet see the dust.

'Let's get to digging,' Drury said. 'We need the extra grub and water.'

Mel changed saddles while Maguire and Drury dug into the loose sand. It seemed to be a losing battle but they got the grave cleared and the girl helped bring out the food-sacks and open the kegs of water. They filled canteens, slaked their thirsts, used a little to wash some of the abrasive grit away from under collars and out of eyes and mouths. Woody took the weary horses back to the dip in the land that led down to the hidden canyon and turned them loose.

By the time they were under way, in the direction Drury knew the third grave site to be, there was a fresh smudge of dust coming up from the south, visible from the top of the lava ridge. The only thing that puzzled Drury about it was that instead of its being large enough to indicate a good-sized squad of *rurales* helping Santiago and his three hard-cases, the dust seemed only to point to a small bunch of riders — half a dozen at the most.

'Might have spare mounts running alongside,' Drury added after telling the others what he had seen. 'But it looks to me like it's just Santiago and his hardcases.'

'Mebbe so he can move faster,' suggested Maguire. 'A small group's better to manage than a whole strung-out bunch of soldiers.'

'Or maybe he just doesn't want witnesses,' Drury said heavily and the girl looked at him sharply, frowning, but nodded gently.

'I — think this may be so!' There was a slight tremor in her voice and then Drury got them moving, scouting on well ahead, for the land had changed its contours since the wind-and-dust storm.

It was going to slow them down.

* * *

'Not taking any trouble to cover their tracks,' announced Cole Fisher, kneeling in the sand. Santiago and the others were sitting their saddles, awaiting his verdict as to which direction the fugitives had taken.

'Which way?' Santiago demanded impatiently.

Fisher pointed, mounting. He grinned

crookedly. 'I'd say we got 'em running scared, Jace.'

'When they are no longer running at all, I will be pleased!' the tall Mexican snapped, spurring his mount forward.

'We gonna leave a sign for the *rurales*?' asked Fisher.

'No!' called Santiago, moving away fast, his spare mount running alongside. 'Let them wander around for a while. After we've taken care of Drury and the others we can find them . . . we don't want them to see the killings.'

Fisher shrugged and spurred after his boss and the others.

* * *

They missed grave three.

There had apparently been more than one windstorm and it was either buried beneath a thick layer of alkali and grit and pumice, or it had been blown flat and faded into the landscape. Drury knew he could find it given time, especially at sundown or sun-up, flat to the ground, when the light was coming in low and strong, yet without glare . . . but that dust cloud behind seemed to be somehow attached to them and moved after them whichever way they rode. Unshakable.

Drury was between a rock and a hard place: to gain distance, he hadn't been stopping to cover their tracks as thoroughly as he would have wished. If he dropped back to hide them so they would be mighty hard for Cole Fisher to find, they would lose ground. Too much ground.

'We'll have to try and make grave four on what we've got,' he announced, making a decision on the spot. 'That means rationing water, giving most to the horses. We've got some oats so that'll swell in their bellies and give 'em the notion that they're fuller than they really are but it won't do 'em a lot of good . . . we'll lose performance. And we'll have to push on after dark — to put more distance between us and Santiago.'

'If that's just that beanpole Mex and his three hardcases, we could lay an ambush,' Maguire suggested but Drury shook his head, indicating old Navarro.

'Rico's doing okay, but he's still old and he's had a helluva lot of bad treatment. We need to get him back to the US so he can tell his story. Once the word gets out that Montegas's men killed Herrera while he was in prison, that's the end of *el Presidente*.'

'Still say we oughta bushwhack 'em,' muttered Maguire, but he didn't give Drury any real argument. He had travelled the wild trails with Drury before and he knew the man had a quicker mind than he had, could plan ahead more easily, recognize more possibilities of danger . . .

So they kept going after dark and gained a good four hours before the condition of the horses forced them to make camp. It was a cold one, and they ate beans straight from the last two cans, less than a half each. They avoided the jerky because it was highly spiced and would only add to their thirst. The horses hadn't had enough of either food or water and spent a restless night, the men having to get up and check their tethering lines constantly.

They were on the trail before sun-up and when the first light did spill a little grey across the land, Drury paused on their climb over a barren ridge and looked back. He swore softly.

Already there was a faint haze of dust out there, right about where he would figure Santiago's group to be . . .

He didn't say anything to the others but he knew they had all seen it for themselves.

Going down the other side of the ridge was quicker but more hazardous and Navarro's ropes slipped so that he hung upside down on his frightened horse and caught a hard knee in the head which left him dizzy for more than an hour. He did not look good and Drury knew they had better find grave four pretty damn quick or they were going to have to bury the old man . . .

They reached grave four in mid-afternoon. It was open and empty — except for the body of one of the Mexicans who had been left to guard the spare horses in the nearby sunken canyon.

In the canyon, they found the bodies of the other two Mexicans, sign that there had been a gun battle, some Indian arrows scattered and broken here and there — and no horses. The tracks were easy to read: a band of Indians had attacked the Mexicans, stolen the horses, robbed the grave of food.

'Owls didn't work,' opined Mel.

'They don't always,' Maguire said in clipped tones. 'Not all Injuns are scared of 'em . . . even those who are, might still take a chance for some decent grub and a bunch of good hosses.'

'There's nothing left we can use,' Drury said grimly, looking around at the hollowed, red-eyed faces staring back at him from behind their masks of alkali and grime. 'We'll have to push on.'

'How far?' croaked Mel.

'Near the pass through the Black Peppers.'

Mel blew out his lips. 'Man! That's a long ways from here — and a long ways from the border!'

'Well, I originally worked out a trail that would keep us close to Gulf coast — believing that Santiago really was trying to bust out Herrera. We need the grub and water and whatever else is in grave five or we're not going to make the border.'

'Sure — but are we gonna make grave five?' queried Woody Maguire, grim-faced.

It was a question all of them were asking themselves.

★   ★   ★

They lost the first horse to a soda sink-hole.

Drury had warned them when crossing the blindingly white soda lake that they could not stray more than a foot either side of the trail they were riding on or they would plunge through the soggy surface into flesh-destroying soda sludge.

They heeded him but Mel, bringing up the rear, dozed in the saddle. Like the others he was near exhaustion and reeling from hunger and thirst. When he jarred awake, his mount had plunged through the crust of the soda lake and was snorting and rearing as the caustic sludge began to eat its flesh.

Mel was thrown on to more solid footing, luckily, but the horse was doomed and Drury threw his rifle to his shoulder and put a bullet through its brain and another when it went down just to make sure it didn't suffer. Mel couldn't get his saddle off but he slid his rifle out of the scabbard and cut the thongs holding his bedroll which was sodden at one end.

They pushed on, Mel walking now because the other horses weren't strong enough to carry double weight. He weaved and staggered and Drury dropped back, told him to grab the stirrup and stay in close against his mount. At least he would have something to guide him.

Mel obeyed, his eyes dulled, his legs moving with effort.

The sun hammered them, the heat coming down on them like physical blows. Their skin felt like parchment at first, then, later, sandpaper. It was an effort to breathe, lungs burning with the desert air. Drury recalled it from six years ago when the old Apache had led him through here.

It was just as bad and they had lost one horse to the soda sink just like this time. But they had crossed and somehow gotten into the shelter of the pass through the *Cerros Negras Pimientas* — the Black Pepper Hills. Drury hadn't even known a pass existed but it had been used for countless years by the Indians. It was waterless, did nothing but cut miles off the run to the Arizona border.

They had almost died, afoot, starving, thirsty, but the Apache had urged him through and then had lit a small fire of dried pepper-bushes and within the hour four wolf-lean Indians had appeared and given them both water and food. Crooked Tree knew them well and he was respected by them but they refused to leave the Black Peppers. They told the old man the way to the border and then faded back into the sierras where they had their hideout . . .

★   ★   ★

Drury himself lost his horse next. It simply folded up after snorting and staggering for more than a quarter of a mile. He stepped out of the saddle as the animal crumpled, grabbed rifle and warbag and empty canteen and fell to one knee, surprised at how weak he was.

He waved the others on, helped Mel to his feet and they stumbled on in the wake of the girl and Navarro and Maguire, supporting each other . . .

By the time the Black Peppers came

in sight — only a dark wavering line in the distance — they were all afoot and, behind them, Santiago's dustcloud was closing in fast . . .

Consuela was helping Navarro and the old man was trying valiantly but looked as if he would collapse at any minute. Woody Maguire, panting like all of them, paused to look behind, then turned to stare at the distant hills.

'Gonna be close,' he rasped and Drury merely nodded, too tired to even talk.

They were on a small rise, exposed to the sun, with only a handful of rocks scattered about the top. Maguire sat down heavily. Drury signalled for him to come along but Maguire shook his head.

'Catch — up.'

'You won't!'

'Don' matter . . . ' Maguire unsheathed his rifle and blew a coating of dust off the action, working the lever stiffly. 'I'll slow 'em down.'

The others had stopped now, waiting

with shoulders sagging, watching Maguire with dulled eyes.

'No, Woody,' grated Drury shaking his head and moving his feet because the motion made him feel dizzy and he had to get a firmer position. 'Won't work. Not enough cover here — they'll surround you . . . '

'Not all of 'em. Go, Dave — I owe you plenty. Never have a better chance to repay you . . . '

'You owe me nothing!' Drury said angrily. 'You've always worked your butt off on the spread — '

'Wastin' time!' cut in Maguire, gesturing to the pursuers who could be seen beneath the edge of the dust cloud. 'I ain't goin' on. Fisher done somethin' to me — inside. I'm all torn up. Been spittin' blood for days . . . Just go, Dave. And, *adios, amigo*. Thanks for everythin'.'

Drury hesitated, waving the others on. Then he glanced at Santiago's fast-approaching band and reached down with his right hand to grip, briefly, with Maguire.

'Been a privilege, Woody.'

'Likewise.'

Drury held the man's hand a little longer then dropped it, flicked a salute from the crumpled brim of his battered hat and swung away, stumbling after the others.

They were almost in the shadow of the Peppers when the first scattered gunshots rattled across the desert.

★ ★ ★

Maguire knew they had seen him. That was OK. He wanted them to see him. They could ride wide around the rise or maybe even ride clear over the top — of him as well as the slopes — but he figured he knew Santiago and those damn hardcases. Though the only one he was truly interested in was Fisher: that son of a bitch had almost turned him inside out. He hadn't felt *right* since taking that beating and he didn't care if he had to die right here, but he was going to square things with the man. He coughed a little blood, wincing.

They scattered now, spreading out and then sweeping in, surrounding the hill as Drury had said they would. He let his gaze slide over Santiago and Quick and Con Conrads, and settled it on Fisher. The man was coming in from the right-hand side. That suited Maguire fine. He took his bead, saw that Fisher had spotted him and saw the man wrench his reins, lying low along his mount's neck.

Woody Maguire grinned against the hot cheekpiece of his Winchester, dropped his sight just a shade, and led Fisher only a little, for the man's horse was plastered with dust on yellowish foam caking its hide and he knew the animal was close to collapse.

Maguire fired, raised his head instantly to see if he had hit target. Fisher didn't move and Maguire's expectant grin died before it was born. Christ, a miss! *No!* Suddenly Cole Fisher reared up in saddle, dropping his rifle, clawing at his left leg and falling heavily. Maguire hooted as he heard the man's scream of agony and he threw the rifle to his shoulder, trying to draw a bead on the man's other knee cap as Cole writhed about in the sand.

There was a ragged volley of shots behind him and Maguire's battered body jerked but he bit back the sob of pain, steadied his aim again as Fisher came to a brief stop and triggered. The hardcase's body spun as if yanked by a wire and his scream was twice as loud this time.

Maguire hollered, feeling pain now, and as he half rose, then was knocked flat by the strike of more lead. His face pushed into the hot sand and he turned his head to one side, coughing, his breath stirring the dust, spraying it with crimson . . . He lay there, unable to move now, straining to listen once more to Cole Fisher's screams.

Then a shadow fell across him and he looked up. The tall Mexican was standing over him, holding a smoking rifle, poking at him with the muzzle.

'Where is the next grave?' Santiago asked, pushing the rifle muzzle against one of Maguire's wounds.

He cried out but only bared bloody teeth.

'Just this side — of — hell!'

His scream of pain mingled with Cole Fisher's cries and when he had stopped gasping, his eyes beginning to roll up, he gasped, 'Through — pass . . . '

Santiago sneered and shot him through the head. Then he walked down to where Conrads and Quick stood looking at Fisher. The man's brutal face was grey with pain under the film of dust. Both his knees were shattered, splinters of bone poking through the erupted flesh and torn trouser cloth.

Santiago shook his head slowly. 'You'll never walk again, Cole . . . too bad . . . '

'Gemme to a — sawbones, Jace! Please . . . '

The Mexican pursed his lips and shook his head once more. Fisher screamed as the man raised the rifle and then lowered it again. 'Sorry, *amigo*. Can't spare the bullet . . . but you'll die anyway.' He turned and walked away, barking at Quick and Conrads to follow. They threw Fisher pitying looks and followed the Mexican as he mounted and rode towards the pass through the Black Pepper Hills.

Cole Fisher screamed, the sound dying away to a sob . . .

★　★　★

Drury knew Maguire was dead by now but forced the knowledge from his mind as he led the others through the pass. They moved better in the shade of the black volcanic rock but when the girl started to lower Navarro to the ground he said, 'No! Keep going . . . right through the pass. The fifth grave's just on the far side.'

'Might be best to rest in — shade,

Dave,' Mel said.

Drury shook his head, took Navarro's other arm and urged the staggering girl on.

'Get the grub and water first. More ammo, too.'

They fell and scraped flesh, Drury using his body to shield the old man as he stumbled. Mel, moving better now, alone, hurried on ahead and located the grave fifty yards to one side of the narrow pass. He tore down the cross, heaved some of the stones aside and began to dig away the sand with sore hands until he uncovered one of the shovels that had been stashed there. He had scooped out enough sand to see the covering timber by the time Drury had seated the girl and Navarro amongst some shady rocks.

The rancher, feeding on renewed energy now, hurried across as well as he could, picked up the second shovel and scraped more sand away from the wood slats.

Neither man had breath to speak as

they uncovered the cache of food and the kegs of water. Drury rolled one across to where Consuela waited, handed her the hammer and screw-driver, indicating that she should open the keg and slake her own and Navarro's thirst.

Mel had taken out some of the sacks of food, brought up an old flour-sack containing six boxes of ammunition and then lifted out a canvas-wrapped, oblong shape.

'More — grub?' he asked, panting.

Drury shook his head and took it, fumbling out his clasp-knife and glanc-ing back at the pass. He could see Santiago riding out ahead of Quick and Conrads as he cut the stitching and tore off the canvas.

The man was impatient to die, it seemed!

Drury opened the cardboard box inside the canvas.

'Judas priest!' exclaimed Mel.

Drury hurriedly spread out several sticks of paper-wrapped dynamite with fuses and detonators already in place.

'Take the grub and make sure the gal keeps her head down — you, too, Mel!' Drury was moving away even as he snapped the orders, making his way back into the pass.

Santiago, entering the far end, saw him, slipped his rifle out of the scabbard and fired two fast shots. The bullets whined from the rock, chips spraying. Quick and Conrads were twenty yards behind but Santiago didn't wait for them. He wanted Drury for himself.

Drury climbed higher, arms feeling like they were wrenching out of their sockets, lungs seared with every gulping breath, boots slipping on the broken rock. The tall Mexican reined up and quit leather in a hurry. He fell but rolled to his feet, starting up after Drury. He paused and fired and the bullets drove Drury into a high crevice.

Here, sheltered from the wind, he lit the first length of fuse with a vesta snapped into flame on a horny thumbnail. He tossed the two sticks of dynamite down the slope.

Santiago saw it falling towards him and spun so fast he fell sprawling, rolling down the slope, bringing up sharply against a rock so that the breath was hammered from his lean body. He buried his head under his arms as the dynamite exploded and black earth erupted and whistled and thudded down the slope, blowing him over the rock. He landed in a bloody heap on the floor of the pass, his clothes shredded.

Drury was already out of the crevice, climbing as high as he could go, seeing Conrads and Quick had reined down, their desert-worn mounts prancing. They yanked hard on their reins, starting to turn, but Drury already had another bundle in the air, smoke trailing from the fuse.

The dynamite exploded above them and blew both men off their horses. One mount was knocked flat but struggled to its feet again, running out of the pass. The men staggered up. Quick still had his gun and Drury saw that it was the shotgun he had seen the man use previously.

He had blood running down his face and one arm was held crookedly but he got the shotgun up and fired both barrels at once. The kick knocked him on his back and the buckshot whistled and hummed from the lava, pieces stinging Drury on the arm and hand. He dropped the dynamite and Conrads fired and the rancher twisted violently as a bullet seared him somewhere high in the chest.

He fell on the rocks, rolled off and landed on a patch of sand. He snatched at his Colt and threw himself down the slope as Conrads ran towards him, shooting. Quick, down on one knee, was trying to fumble out a fresh load of shells for his shotgun.

Drury hurled himself over a low rock, twisting in mid-air, thumbing the gun hammer twice. Conrads stopped in mid-stride and he swayed, legs beginning to buckle. Drury hit the ground and rolled one more time, landing on his belly, shooting at Conrads. The shot knocked the man down hard and he tried to get up but fell flat on his face: the only movement was his hands clawing into the dust until the fingers straightened out and were still.

Drury wrenched around, gasping at the pain that tore across his chest, saw Quick straightening, fumbling with three or four shotgun shells in his hand as he tried to manipulate two into the gun's breech. The rancher had only one shot left and there was no time to take aim. He triggered and there was an explosion — or three or four so close together it sounded like one — and when the smoke cleared there was only raw meat where Quick had been standing and the shotgun was a lump of twisted metal and splintered wood . . .

Ears ringing, Drury climbed wearily to his feet and fumbled to reload his six-gun as he staggered his way back to where Santiago lay on the floor of the pass. He paused to examine his wound but it was shallow, though bleeding considerably. He wadded a kerchief over it and moved on.

He saw Mel hurrying out of the rocks where he had sheltered Consuela and Navarro and then he dropped to one knee beside Santiago. The man was not a pretty sight when Drury heaved him on to his back.

But the eyes still had hatred burning in them as the tall Mexican looked up through the mask of blood.

'End of the line, Santiago. I've enough dynamite left to seal the pass so even if the *rurales* come after us we'll be back in Arizona before they find a way through or around these hills . . . Montegas is finished now.'

Santiago managed to call him a filthy name in Spanish.

'You know, you've always reminded me of someone,' Drury said slowly. 'You kin of Montegas?'

The eyes blazed. 'Cousin!' the man gasped.

'So that's why you worked so hard at this. You were gonna divide Mexico between you.'

Santiago said nothing.

'You had Fisher grab Herrera from the train he thought a US Senator had laid on for him. But what was Montegas trying to torture out of him . . . ?'

Santiago bared his teeth. 'Ev — everyone thought the General was such a fine — fine hero!' He tried to laugh but it turned to a hacking cough and blood sprayed over Drury's dusty boots. 'But — but he made sure his future was well taken care of . . . ' He gasped and wheezed. 'Mexico is not noted for having long-serving *presidentes* so Herrera stole half the treasury and spirited it away to — somewhere! They say he personally killed the men who helped him hide it, just like an old-time pirate. He — he took the secret of its hiding-place with him to the grave . . . '

Drury was silent. It didn't surprise him but there would be a hell of a lot of people who *would* be surprised to know that General Carlos Herrera, Hero of the Revolution, was nothing more than a common thief.

One of them would be Consuela . . .

But she didn't have to know what Santiago had told him and Mel was only now coming in so he hadn't heard. Santiago was breathing his last as Drury stood and turned towards Mel Roberts.

'One more chore to do, Mel — seal up the pass. Then we go get the spare horses in the hidden canyon and with any luck we'll be in Arizona by sundown tomorrow.'

'Suits me. We gonna turn Navarro over to the law?'

'To someone who'll want to listen to his story. He'll recover, I guess, and make a new home north of the border.'

Mel nodded. 'What about Consuela?'

Drury didn't answer as they started climbing up to the crevice where he had dropped the rest of the ready-fused dynamite. They searched for it and found it and planted it in a strategic position and were lighting the fuse when Drury said.

'Guess she'll go back to Montez. Nothing to keep her in Arizona.'

Mel glanced at him quickly.

There was sadness and disappointment in Drury's voice.

As they ran to get away from the coming explosion, Mel panted,

'Aw, you never know, Dave. You just never know!'

THE END

We do hope that you have enjoyed reading this large print book.

Did you know that all of our titles are available for purchase?

We publish a wide range of high quality large print books including:
Romances, Mysteries, Classics
General Fiction
Non Fiction and Westerns

Special interest titles available in large print are:
The Little Oxford Dictionary
Music Book, Song Book
Hymn Book, Service Book

Also available from us courtesy of Oxford University Press:
Young Readers' Dictionary
(large print edition)
Young Readers' Thesaurus
(large print edition)

For further information or a free brochure, please contact us at:
Ulverscroft Large Print Books Ltd.,
The Green, Bradgate Road, Anstey,
Leicester, LE7 7FU, England.
Tel: (00 44) **0116 236 4325**
Fax: (00 44) **0116 234 0205**

DEAD IS FOR EVER

Amy Sadler

After rescuing Hope Bennett from the clutches of two trailbums, Sam Carver made a serious mistake. He killed one of the outlaws, and reckoned on collecting the bounty on Lew Daggett. But catching Sam off-guard, Daggett made off with the girl, leaving Sam for dead. However, he was only grazed and once he came to, he set out in search of Hope. When he eventually found her, he was forced into a dramatic showdown with his life on the line.